# SUPER EXPERT
# PHYSICS QUIZ

# SUPER EXPERT PHYSICS QUIZ

Vijaya Khandurie

RUPA

Published by
Rupa Publications India Pvt. Ltd 2005
7/16, Ansari Road, Daryaganj
New Delhi 110002

*Sales centres:*

Allahabad Bengaluru Chennai
Hyderabad Jaipur Kathmandu
Kolkata Mumbai

ISBN: 978-81-291-0850-0

Fifth impression 2015

10 9 8 7 6 5

The moral right of the author has been asserted.

**To**

Late Sh. Narinder Singh Sistani
(21.06.1925 - 06.07.2005)
One of the finest persons I have come across.
Besides being a well-known lawyer, he was a
keen sportsperson,
an avid reader having great interest in educa-
tion, a strict disciplinarian,
and above all a perfect gentleman.

# CONTENTS

# PREFACE

Once Niels Bohr, the famous Danish physicist remarked, 'An expert is a man who has made all the mistakes, which can be made, in a very narrow field.'

So the experts are also prone to make mistakes!

Werner Heisenberg, German physicist, has also linked expertise with mistakes: 'An expert is someone who knows some of the worst mistakes that can be made in his subject, and how to avoid them.'

So the quiz-solvers should feel 'greatly' relieved!

In each of the twenty-five interesting chapters, the quiz questions follow the rule 'from simple to complex'. Simple questions for the expert and difficult ones for the super expert.

Every chapter is preceded by a suitable quotation. Once Thomas Love Peacock, the famous British novelist said: 'A book that furnishes no quotations is, me judice, no book—it is a plaything.'

The aim of quizzing is to improve the capacity for critical thinking, reasoning, logical deduction and create awareness among the young minds.

The role of a student in the process of problem-solving has now evolved from a receptor of information to a researcher of information, from a guided experimenter to an experimental designer, from a responder to ideas to an initiator of work, from a passive receiver to an active participant, and from a minor evaluator to a major one.

I hope quiz lovers will enjoy solving the questions set in the book.

## ACKNOWLEDGEMENTS

While selecting and framing these quiz questions, I had to consult a large number of books and encyclopaedias. I am grateful to their writers for extending my knowledge.

I am also indebted to the photography division of the American Centre, New Delhi, for providing me some photographs used in the book.

I also thank Mr Mayank Aggarwal of Graphic World for helping me with the diagrams.

Finally, I am grateful to my wife Manju Khandurie for giving me support in this endeavour.

# HISTORY OF PHYSICS

A study of history shows that civilisations that abandoned the quest for knowledge are doomed to disintegration.

– BERNARD LOWELL

1. Who was the first pre-Socratic philosopher to suggest that matter could neither be created nor destroyed?
   (a) Democritus
   (b) Parmenides
   (c) Empedocles
   (d) Pythagoras

2. Which Greek philosopher suggested that the material world was composed of four basic elements: air, water, fire, and earth?
   (a) Empedocles
   (b) Heraclitus
   (c) Plato
   (d) Anaximander

3. Which philosopher gave the idea for the first time that all matter was made up of minute indivisible particles called *atomos*?
   (a) Lucretius
   (b) Epicurus
   (c) Leucippus
   (d) Democritus

4. Who, among the following, was the first person to design models of flying machines?
   (a) Wright brothers
   (b) Montgolfier brothers
   (c) Leonardo da Vinci
   (d) Otto Lilienthal

5. An important event took place in the year 1665. Which of the following is it? ·
   (a) The discovery of Newtonian laws of gravitation
   (b) The discovery of Hooke's law
   (c) The discovery of Pascal's law
   (d) Ole Römer measured the velocity of light

6. Who in the year 1643 was the first to create vacuum above the liquid?
   (a) Robert Hooke          (b) Blaise Pascal
   (c) Otto von Guericke     (d) Evangelista Torricelli

7. In which year did Otto von Guericke demonstrate his famous Magdeburg experiment dealing with vacuum?
   (a) 1642                  (b) 1652
   (c) 1662                  (d) 1672

8. When Anders Celsius invented the thermometer in the year 1742, he used $0^0$ for the boiling point and $100^0$ for the freezing point of water. A year later, who among the following, swapped the points and switched over to the system that we use today?
   (a) Francisco Grimaldi    (b) David Gregory
   (c) Jean Pierre Christin  (d) Anders Celsius

9. Who in 1786 invented the gold leaf electroscope?
   (a) Abraham Bennet        (b) Henry Cavendish
   (c) Luigi Galvani         (d) Georg von Klist

10. Who, among the following, was the first to attacl Newton's corpuscular theory of light?
    (a) Albert Einstein      (b) Christiaan Huygens
    (c) James Clerk Maxwell  (d) Thomas Young

11. Apart from inventing the telephone, Alexander Graham Bell also patented a device to transmit message using light rays, an idea far ahead of his time. What was this device called?
    (a) Photophone
    (b) Optical fibre
    (c) Television
    (d) Laser

12. In which year did Luigi Galvani discover, albeit accidentally, the action of electricity on the muscles of a dissected frog?
    (a) 1751
    (b) 1761
    (c) 1771
    (d) 1781

13. The first practical way to store static electricity was the Leyden jar. Who in 1746 invented it?
    (a) Allessandra Volta
    (b) Lord Leyden
    (c) Pieter von Musschenenbrock and Cuneus of Leyden University
    (d) William of Orange

14. Who in 1749 developed a method for making an artificial magnet?
    (a) Charles Du Fay
    (b) John Canton
    (c) John Robinson
    (d) Stephen Gray

15. In 1752, Benjamin Franklin conducted the famous kite experiment. What did it suggest?
    (a) Lightning is a form of electricity.
    (b) Clouds consist of charged particles.
    (c) Pressure is low in the upper atmosphere.
    (d) Electricity requires a conductor to flow.

16. Which famous Danish physicist in 1675 measured the speed of light?
    - (a) Bradley
    - (b) Fizeau
    - (c) Foucault
    - (d) Römer

17. What did Sir William Herschel discover in the year 1800?
    - (a) Infra-red radiation
    - (b) The planet Uranus
    - (c) Ultraviolet radiation
    - (d) A process of photography

18. In which year did Georg Simon Ohm formulate Ohm's law?
    - (a) 1815
    - (b) 1820
    - (c) 1827
    - (d) 1835

19. Robert Brown discovered 'Brownian Motion' in the year 1827. He was basically a:
    - (a) zoologist
    - (b) botanist
    - (c) chemist
    - (d) physicist

20. Who introduced the term 'electron' and estimated its charge?
    - (a) George Stoney
    - (b) J.J. Thomson
    - (c) G.P. Thomson
    - (d) Eugene Goldstein

# 2

## INVASION OF IDEAS

A stand can be made against invasion by an army; no stand can be made against invasion by an idea.

– Victor Hugo

1. Who among the following philosophers conjectured that if the moon did not move, it would fall upon the earth?
   (a) Aristotle       (b) Socrates
   (c) Anaxagoras      (d) Heraclitus

2. 'Sun is the central body around which the earth and other planets revolve.' Who propounded this idea?
   (a) Johannes Kepler    (b) Nicolaus Copernicus
   (c) Tycho Brahe       (d) Epicurus

3. Who said, 'A bird is an instrument working according to the mathematical laws'?
   (a) Leonardo da Vinci   (b) Pythagoras
   (c) Euclid           (d) René Descartes

4. Which Greek philosopher formulated the idea: 'A body when immersed in a fluid displaces a weight of the fluid equal to its own volume'?
   (a) Aristarchus       (b) Antisthenes
   (c) Apollonius       (d) Archimedes

5.  Who was the first to suggest: 'A planet moves most quickly when it is closest to the sun, but slows down as it moves farther away.'?
    (a) Tycho Brahe              (b) Galileo Galilei
    (c) Johannes Kepler          (d) Edwin Hubble

6.  'Regular strokes of the pendulum could be utilised in the accurate measurement of time.' Who was the first to advance this idea?
    (a) Evangelista Torricelli   (b) Galileo Galilei
    (c) John Wallis              (d) Christiaan Huygens

7.  Who said, 'All falling bodies, irrespective of the size, descend with the same speed.'?
    (a) Galileo Galilei          (b) Isaac Newton
    (c) Blaise Pascal            (d) Aristotle

8.  Who formulated the idea: 'Every particle in the universe attracts every other with a force that gets stronger with mass and weaker with distance.'?
    (a) Charles de Coulomb       (b) Henry Cavendish
    (c) Isaac Newton            (d) Guillaume Amontous

9.  Who contemplated for the first time the idea, 'A freely floating magnet orients itself in the north–south direction.'?
    (a) William Gilbert          (b) Edmund Gunter
    (c) Christian Oersted        (d) Robert Norman

10. Who gave this idea for the first time: 'Electricity flows through space from a heated metal.'?
    (a) Lee De Forest            (b) John Ambrose Fleming
    (c) Thomas Alva Edison       (d) Owen Richardson

11. Who, among the following, was the first to think, 'The period of oscillation of a pendulum is independent of its amplitude.'?
    (a) Giordano Bruno    (b) Galileo Galilei
    (c) Johann Lambert    (d) Brook Taylor

12. Name the physicist who theorised, 'An orbiting electron emits light when its orbit shrinks.'?
    (a) James Clerk Maxwell    (b) Ernest Rutherford
    (c) Victor de Broglie    (d) Niels Bohr

13. 'Moving particles have wave characteristics' was the idea first proposed by:
    (a) Erwin Schrödinger    (b) Victor de Broglie
    (c) Arnold Summerfeld    (d) Max Born

14. Who suggested that light is made up of packets of energy known as photons?
    (a) Albert Einstein    (b) Max Planck
    (c) P.A.M. Dirac    (d) Hermann Helmholtz

15. 'Electrons revolve round the nucleus in well-defined orbits, like planets revolve round the sun', was the brain-child of which scientist?
    (a) Ernest Rutherford    (b) Max Born
    (c) Arnold Sommerfeld    (d) Niels Bohr

16. 'Speed of light is the same no matter how it is measured' was first contemplated by:
    (a) Armand Fizeau    (b) Jean Foucault
    (c) A.A. Michelson    (d) Albert Einstein

17. Who, among the following, was the first to suggest that matter and energy are interchangeable?
    (a) George Fitzgerald    (b) Ludwig Boltzmann
    (c) Albert Einstein    (d) Auguste Lumiere

18. The concept of atomic number was first proposed by:
    (a) Frederick Soddy
    (b) Henry Moseley
    (c) James Chadwick
    (d) Ludwig Prandtl

19. Who, among the following, formulated the idea, 'The farther away a galaxy is, the faster it is moving'?
    (a) L. Humason
    (b) Henrietta Levitt
    (c) Allan Sandge
    (d) Edwin Hubble

20. Who conceived this basic fact: 'Physical conditions remaining unaltered, the electric current in a conductor is proportional to the potential difference between its ends'?
    (a) Gustav Kirchhoff
    (b) Carey Foster
    (c) Georg Simon Ohm
    (d) André-Marie Ampère

# 3

## IDEAS IN ACTION

Edison, whose inventions did as much as any to add to our material convenience, wasn't what we would call a scientist at all, but a supreme 'do-it-yourself' man – the successor to Benjamin Franklin.

– KENNETH CLARK

1. Name the device which converts electric energy into mechanical energy:
   (a) alternator      (b) transformer
   (c) dynamo      (d) motor

2. What is the name of the instrument that measures and records the relative humidity of the air?
   (a) hygroscope      (b) hygrograph
   (c) hygrometer      (d) hygrister

3. Which device controls heating and cooling to maintain a desired temperature?
   (a) cryostat      (b) thermostat
   (c) thermister      (d) thermite

4. Name the barometer which does not contain a liquid:
   (a) Aneroid barometer      (b) Fortin's barometer
   (c) Mercury barometer      (d) Barostat

5. A projection lantern used for transparencies or for opaque objects is called:
   - (a) episcope
   - (b) epidiascope
   - (c) slide projector
   - (d) overhead projector

6. A thermometer for measuring very low temperature is called:
   - (a) pyrometer
   - (b) bolometer
   - (c) cryometer
   - (d) platinum resistant thermometer

7. An instrument for measuring focal length of a lens is called:
   - (a) focometer
   - (b) goniometer
   - (c) heliometer
   - (d) spherometer

8. Name the device for detecting and measuring small amount of thermal energy:
   - (a) barretter
   - (b) pyrometer
   - (c) pyranometer
   - (d) bolometer

9. The underwater analogue of microphone is:
   - (a) sonobuoy
   - (b) megaphone
   - (c) hydrophone
   - (d) acoustic torpedo

10. Which of the following is most suitable for measuring very high temperatures?
    - (a) thermocouple
    - (b) pyrometer
    - (c) thermoelectric thermometer
    - (d) platinum resistance thermometer

11. What is the technique for reproducing a stereoscopic image without a lens or a camera?
    (a) thermography          (b) chromatography
    (c) stereography          (d) holography

12. A device for recording epoch of an event is:
    (a) chronoscope           (b) chronograph
    (c) chronometer           (d) metronome

13. What is the device for obtaining a parallel beam of radiation?
    (a) collimator            (b) colirimeter
    (c) calorimeter           (d) coulometer

14. Name the device used to produce a visual image of rapidly varying electrical quantities:
    (a) oscillogram           (b) oscillograph
    (c) oscillator            (d) oscilloscope

15. What is that device which records the electric activities of the brain?
    (a) Electroretinograph    (b) Electrophoretogram
    (c) Electroencephalogram  (d) Electroencephalograph

16. Which instrument measures vapour pressure?
    (a) Bourdon gauge         (b) manometer
    (c) manocryometer         (d) tonometer

17. Name the device for measuring the intensity of sound waves in fluids?
    (a) acoustic radiator     (b) acoustic radiometer
    (c) acoustic spectrometer (d) acoustic amplifier

18. A flexible device of connective links used to transmit power is called:
    (a) gear drive          (b) belt drive
    (c) chain drive         (d) block and tackle

19. Which device, based on the phenomenon of thermionic emission, is used to convert heat energy directly to electric energy?
    (a) thermionic tube
    (b) thermocouple
    (c) thermionic power generator
    (d) thermo-electric generator

20. Ultrasonic frequencies may be generated by the following devices:
    I.   Galton whistle
    II.  Hartmann generator
    III. Piezoelectric oscillator

    Which combination is correct?
    (a) I & II only          (b) I & III only
    (c) II & III only        (d) I, II and III

# 4

## MEASUREMENT AND UNITS

There is no 'royal road' to geometry.

– EUCLID

1. What is the S.I. unit of pressure?
   - (a) atmosphere
   - (b) bar
   - (c) torr
   - (d) pascal

2. Which of the following is not the basic unit of measurement?
   - (a) radian
   - (b) kelvin
   - (c) mole
   - (d) candela

3. What does parsec measure?
   - (a) astronomical distances
   - (b) very small distances
   - (c) time
   - (d) the arc of a circle

4. What is the unit of surface tension?
   - (a) Newton
   - (b) Newton-metre
   - (c) Newton per metre
   - (d) Newton per square metre

5. One Ångström is equal to
   (a) $10^{-8}$ m                    (b) $10^{-10}$ m
   (c) $10^8$ m                       (d) $10^{10}$ m

6. Which, among the following, is not a unit of force?
   (a) dyne                          (b) sthene
   (c) stilb                         (d) newton

7. One degree ( $1°$ ) is equal to:
   (a) $\pi/$ 360 rad                (b) $\pi/$ 180 rad
   (c) $\pi/$ 90 rad                 (d) $\pi/$ 60 rad

8. Lux is the unit of which physical quantity?
   (a) luminance                     (b) luminous intensity
   (c) luminous flux                 (d) illumination

9. One light-year is equal to:
   (a) $5.8785 \times 10^{12}$ miles  (b) $9.4607 \times 10^{15}$ metres
   (c) 0.307 parsec                  (d) all the above

10. Unit of pressure in vacuum technology is:
    (a) mmHg                         (b) millibar
    (c) torr                         (d) atm

11. Unit of time equal to the period of rotation of earth is:
    (a) day                          (b) solar day
    (c) mean solar day               (d) sidereal day

12. One litre is not equivalent to:
    (a) $10^6$ mm$^3$                (b) $10^3$ cm$^3$
    (c) $10^{-3}$ m$^3$             (d) $1^3$ dm

13. Which, among the following, is the smallest unit of length?
    (a) angström                     (b) fermi
    (c) micron                       (d) nanometre

14. Magnitude is a measure of:
    (a) direction
    (b) stellar brightness
    (c) enthalpy
    (d) entropy

15. What is the S.I. unit of electric field strength?
    (a) Volt per metre
    (b) Newton per metre
    (c) Joule per metre
    (d) Ampère per metre

16. Which of the following systems of units was replaced by the S.I. units in 1954?
    (a) C.G.S. units
    (b) F.P.S. units
    (c) M.K.S. units
    (d) GIORGI units

17. The unit of frequency is hertz. What is the name given to the unit of frequency equal to $10^{12}$ hertz?
    (a) Fresnel
    (b) Lloyd
    (c) Planck
    (d) Young

18. What is measured in the Richter Scale? The intensity of:
    (a) volcanoes
    (b) typhoons
    (c) storms
    (d) earthquakes

19. What does an odometer measure?
    (a) force
    (b) smell
    (c) speed
    (d) purity of milk

20. The S.I. unit of dose equivalent is:
    (a) bequerel
    (b) curie
    (c) gray
    (d) sievert

# 5

# SYMBOLIC PHYSICS: FROM A TO Z

Number constitutes the only universal language.

– NATHANIEL WEST

1. The unit of temperature is not denoted by:
   (a) T                    (b) K
   (c) °F                   (d °R

2. What does the prefix 'giga' mean?
   (a) $10^{-9}$            (b) $10^9$
   (c) $10^{-15}$           (d) $10^{15}$

3. One nano-second means:
   (a) 0.000 000 001s
   (b) 0.000 000 000 001s
   (c) 0.000 000 000 000 001s
   (d) 0.000 000 000 000 000 001s

4. Symbol for hectare is:
   (a) h                    (b) H
   (c) ha                   (d) Ha

5. Which elementary particle is represented by γ ?
   (a) neutrino             (b) photon
   (c) meson                (d) quark

6. 'C' is the symbol for the unit of:
   (a) electric current      (b) electrical capacitance
   (c) electric charge      (d) electric conductance

7. Which of the following diagrams represents a variable resistance?

   (a)

   (b)

   (c)

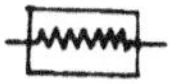

   (d)

8. In the formula 'p = mv', what does 'p' signify?
   (a) pressure      (b) power
   (c) potential      (d) momentum

9. What does the Greek alphabet 'η' represent?
   (a) emissivity      (b) coefficient of viscocity
   (c) permeability      (d) entropy

10. Among the popular abbreviated terms LF, HF, VHF, UHF, what does 'F' indicate?
    (a) frequency      (b) force
    (c) field      (d) function

11. 'pF' means:
    (a) forward power dissipation
    (b) product of momentum and force
    (c) foot poundal
    (d) picofarad

12. Faraday's laws of electrolysis are symbolised by the equation 'm = Zct'. What does 'Z' represent?
    (a) electric field strength
    (b) electromagnetic mass
    (c) electrochemical equivalent
    (d) electrokinetic potential

13. Among the following diagrams, which symbolises the tuning capacitor?

(a)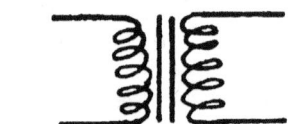

(b)

(c)

(d)

14. One kilobyte is equal to:
    (a) 1000 bytes          (b) 512 bytes
    (c) 1024 bytes          (d) 1052 bytes

15. What does the following graphic symbol represent?

    (a) Air core transformer   (b) Autotransformer
    (c) Iron core transformer  (d) Power transformer

16. What is 'ELINT'?
    (a) European Linked International Television
    (b) Electronic Laboratory Instruments at Normal
        Temperature
    (c) Extremely Light Integrated Nuclear Terminal
    (d) Electronic Intelligence

17. What is the acronym for 'radar and television aid navigation'?
    (a) RATAN          (b) ratan
    (c) RTV            (d) RATN

18. The name of the number $10^{100}$ is:
    (a) centimillion          (b) zillion
    (c) googol                (d) ctollion

19. Our neighbouring spiral galaxy in Andromeda is catalogued as 'M 31' What does 'M' indicate?
    (a) messier               (b) mercator
    (c) magnitude             (d) medium

20. 'Z' is not:
    (a) zeta potential        (b) impedance
    (c) atomic number         (d) section modulus

# 6

# CLASSICAL MECHANICS

If I have seen further it is by standing on the shoulders of giants.

— Isaac Newton

1.  Which of the following combinations is true about the mass of a body according to Newton?
    I.   Mass is the quantity of matter contained in a body.
    II.  Mass is represented by the relation, mass = force/velocity.
    III. Mass is always conserved.
    IV.  Mass of a body is the ratio of its weight to the acceleration due to gravity at a particular place.

    (a) I, II, and III only      (b) I, III, and IV only
    (c) I, II, and IV only      (d) I, II, III, and IV

2.  According to Newtonian mechanics:
    I.   mass is a quantitative measure of a body's inertia.
    II.  mass is a measure of the attraction of one body to another.
    III. inertial and gravitational masses are equivalent.
    IV.  mass is invariant.

    Which combination is correct?
    (a) I, III, and IV only      (b) I, II, and III only
    (c) I, II, and IV only      (d) I, II, III, and IV

3. Inertia is the property of a body which preserves its state of rest or uniform motion in a straight line. The following factors tell more about inertia:

   I. Greater the mass of a body, greater is its inertia.
   II. Greater the inertia of a body, lesser will be the acceleration produced by a given force.
   III. The law of inertia is the same as Newton's first law of motion.

   Which combination is true?
   (a) I, II, and III        (b) I, and II only
   (c) I, and III only       (d) II, and III only

4. Two fully blown balloons are suspended as shown in the diagram. A stream of air is passed in between the balloons. What will happen to the balloons?

   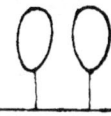

   (a) They will come closer    (b) They will go apart
   (c) There will be no change   (d) They will go up

5. A cricket ball after being hit by a batsman returns to the ground sometime later after having described a parabolic path. Which of the following factors remains unaltered?

   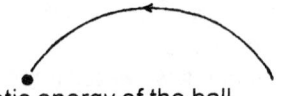

   (a) The kinetic energy of the ball
   (b) The potential energy of the ball
   (c) The horizontal component of the velocity of the ball
   (d) The vertical component of the velocity of the ball

6. Which of the following is not a vector quantity?
   (a) retardation        (b) displacement
   (c) velocity           (d) time

7.  Consider the following situations:
    I.   A car moves with uniform speed on a smooth level road.
    II.  A body moves with uniform speed in a circular path.
    III. A labourer carries bricks on his head from one place to another on a smooth level road.

    Which combination justifies that the work is being done?
    (a) II only                    (b) I and II only
    (c) in all the cases           (d) in none of the cases

8.  A ball of mass 'm' strikes a ball with a velocity 'v' and then its speed is reversed. What is the change in the momentum of the ball?

    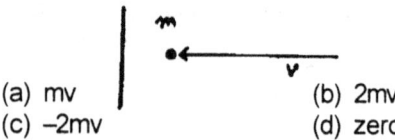

    (a) mv                         (b) 2mv
    (c) –2mv                       (d) zero

9.  At what angle should an athlete throw his javelin to attain the maximum range?
    (a) 30°                        (b) 45°
    (c) 60°                        (d) 75°

10. From Newton's laws of motion, one can infer that:
    I.   Newton's first law describes the motion of a body free of external forces.
    II.  Newton's second law relates force to motion.
    III. Newton's third law is a statement about forces in motion.
    IV.  Newton's third law leads to the principle of conservation of momentum.

    Which combination is true?
    (a) I,II and III only           (b) I, II and IV only
    (c) II, III and IV only         (d) I,II,III and IV

11. What drives a nail into wood when struck by a hammer?
    (a) force                    (b) impulse
    (c) momentum                 (d) acceleration

12. Impulse is:
    I.   the total effect of a force
    II.  the product of average force and the time for which
         the force acts
    III. equal to the total change in momentum

    Which combination is false?
    (a) I only                   (b) II only
    (c) III only                 (d) none of these

13. Which combination of the following statements is
    wrong?
    I.   A body can have a constant speed but a varying
         velocity.
    II.  A body can have a constant velocity but a varying
         speed.
    III. A body can have a zero velocity and finite
         accelertation.

    (a) I only                   (b) II only
    (c) III only                 (d) None of these

14. What is not true about momentum?
    (a) It is the product of the mass and the velocity of the
        body.
    (b) It is a vector quantity whose direction is same as
        that of the velocity.
    (c) Its physical dimension is $MLT^{-2}$.
    (d) Its S.I. unit is kilogram metre per second.

15. Think about the following statements about momentum:
    I.   The rate at which momentum changes is equal to the force applied.
    II.  The mass of the particle times its acceleration is equal to the rate of change of its momentum.
    III. The change of momentum of a body is equal to the Impulse applied on it.

    Which combination is wrong?
    (a) II only                    (b) III only
    (c) I,II and III               (d) none of these

16. The analog of moment of inertia in a linear motion is:
    (a) mass                       (b) couple
    (c) torque                     (d) momentum

17. A rectangular block with edges ABCDEFGH is placed on the ground in various positions of its base. Which face of the body will exert maximum pressure on the ground?

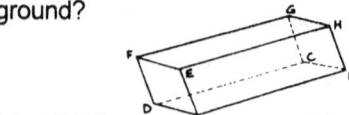

    (a) ADFE                       (b) ABCD
    (c) ABHE                       (d) it is the same all over

18. Water is allowed to come out of a hole 'P' which is exactly at the middle of the wall of a tank of height 'H'. At what distance from the tank, the water stream strikes the ground?

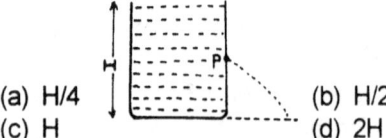

    (a) H/4                        (b) H/2
    (c) H                          (d) 2H

19. In which of the following cases the level of liquid increases when a piece of ice melts completely?
    (a) A piece of cork is embedded inside an ice block which floats in water.
    (b) A piece of ice floats in water.
    (c) A piece of ice floats in a liquid of specific gravity 1.2.
    (d) A piece of ice sinks in a liquid of specific gravity 0.7.

20. The following graph shows the variation of volume with temperature in case of water.

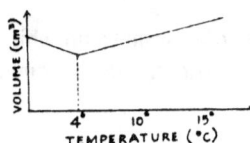

What does the graph indicate?
    (a) Volume increases with temperature
    (b) Volume decreases with temperature
    (c) Density of water is minimum at 4°C
    (d) Density of water is maximum at 4°C

# 7

# FIELDS AND FORCES

Electric force is defined as something which causes motion oı electric charge: an electric charge is something which exerts electric force.

– Arthur Eddington

1. Which of the following is not the fundamental force of nature?
   (a) weak nuclear force
   (b) strong nuclear interaction
   (c) cohesive force
   (d) electromagnetic force

2. A fictitious outward force on a particle rotating about an axis is:
   (a) centrifugal force      (b) centripetal force
   (c) tangential force       (d) Coriolis force

3. The separation of cream during the churning of milk is due to:
   (a) centrifugal force      (b) centripetal force
   (c) frictional force       (d) viscous drag

4. Which is not the unit of force among the following?
   (a) dyne                   (b) Newton
   (c) pound                  (d) kilogram-weight

5. 'Weight' of a body may have the following attributes:
   I.   It is the gravitational force acting on a body at the earth's surface.
   II.  It is independent of the mass of the body.
   III. The body is weightless during the free fall.
   IV.  It is different at different places on earth's surface.

   Which combination is correct?
   (a) I and III only            (b) I, III and IV only
   (c) I, II and III only        (d) I, II, III and IV

6. The coulombian forces are responsible for binding:
   I.   an atom to an atom to form a molecule.
   II.  an electron to a nucleus to form an atom.
   III. a molecule to a molecule to form a solid or a liquid.

   Which combination is correct ?
   (a) I and II only             (b) I and III only
   (c) II and III only           (d) I, II and III

7. The most universal of all the basic forces in nature is:
   (a) gravitational force
   (b) electromagnetic force
   (c) weak nuclear interaction
   (d) strong nuclear interaction

8. The forces that hold pieces of matter together and give them strength are called:
   (a) elastic forces            (b) adhesive forces
   (c) cohesive forces           (d) frictional forces

9. The inward force required to keep a satellite moving in a circular orbit is:
   (a) centrifugal force         (b) centripetal force
   (c) gravitational force       (d) aerodynamic force

10. 'Action at a distance' is revealed most prominently in:
    (a) gravitational force     (b) electric force
    (c) magnetic force          (d) electromagnetic force

11. What is impulse?
    (a) A large force acting for a long period.
    (b) A large force acting for a short period.
    (c) A small force acting for a long period.
    (d) A small force acting for a short period.

12. Three forces are in equilibrium, then each force is:
    (a) equal to the sum of the remaining two.
    (b) equal to the difference of the remaining two.
    (c) greater than the sum of the remaining two.
    (d) greater than the difference of the remaining two.

13. 'If three forces act on a particle in equilibrium, each is proportional to the sine of the angle between the other two'. This is known as:
    (a) Law of triangle of forces
    (b) Law of parallelogram of forces
    (c) Lamy's theorem
    (d) Law of polygon of forces

14. A system of two equal and opposite parallel forces is called:
    (a) couple                  (b) moment
    (c) torque                  (d) torsion

15. The force responsible in the formation of the galaxies is:
    (a) strong attractive force (b) inter-galactic force
    (c) gravitational force     (d) magnetic force

16. The force that tends to minimise the area of a liquid surface is known as:
    (a) surface tension
    (b) intermolecular force
    (c) viscous force
    (d) adhesive force

17. A force that acts only for a short duration but large enough to cause a change in momentum on the body it acts is called:
    (a) hadronic force
    (b) leptonic force
    (c) drag force
    (d) impulsive force

18. Which of the following statements is not true about gravitational force?
    (a) It is the weakest force in nature.
    (b) It is the most universal of all the natural forces.
    (c) It is the same as the force of gravity.
    (d) The gravitational force between two bodies decreases as the distance between them increases.

19. Consider the following statements about friction:
    I.   Friction is a kind of cohesive force.
    II.  Friction is the force that cannot start moving a body.
    III. Friction is a dissipative force, i.e. it produces heat that is not mechanical.

    Which combination is *not* true?
    (a) I only
    (b) II only
    (c) III only
    (d) none of the above

20. When a body is totally or partially immersed in a liquid, an upward force, called upthrust, acts from the liquid, which depends on:
    (a) weight of liquid that is displaced.
    (b) weight of the body that is immersed.
    (c) volume of the body that is immersed.
    (d) amount of liquid that is displaced.

# 8

# ENERGY

Nature and Nature's laws lay hid in night:
God said, 'Let Newton be' and all was light.

– Alexander Pope

1. In a steam engine:
   - (a) heat energy is converted into mechanical energy.
   - (b) chemical energy is converted into heat energy.
   - (c) mechanical energy is converted into heat energy.
   - (d) chemical energy is converted into mechanical energy.

2. A body when in motion possesses:
   - (a) potential energy
   - (b) kinetic energy
   - (c) mechanical energy
   - (d) translational energy

3. By which mode of transmission, heat energy is received on earth from the sun?
   - (a) conduction
   - (b) convection
   - (c) radiation
   - (d) all the above

4. Which among the following physical quantities has the same unit and dimension as that of energy?
   - (a) power
   - (b) work
   - (c) pressure
   - (d) force

5. Which of the following is not an example of potential energy?
   (a) A wound clock-spring.
   (b) A body at rest at some height from the ground.
   (c) A vibrating pendulum at its maximum displacement from the mean position.
   (d) A vibrating pendulum when it is just passing through the mean position.

6. Consider the following facts about energy:
   I.   Electrical energy can be stored in a capacitor to be recovered on its discharge.
   II.  It is stored in the electromagnetic radiations in electric and magnetic fields.
   III. In a closed system, the total energy is variable.
   IV.  Potential energy is stored in a body when it changes its configuration.

   Which of the following combinations is true?
   (a) I, II and III          (b) I, II and IV
   (c) I, III and IV          (d) II, III and IV

7. What type of energy conversion takes place when a compressed spring is released?
   (a) Potential energy to kinetic energy
   (b) Kinetic energy to potential energy
   (c) Molecular energy to potential energy
   (d) Potential energy to molecular energy

8. Which of these is not a unit of energy?
   (a) Kilowatt hour          (b) Foot-poundal force
   (c) Watt per second        (d) Erg

9. Which of the following statements is wrong?
   (a) In a battery, chemical energy is converted into electric energy.
   (b) In a steam engine, heat energy is converted into mechanical work.
   (c) In electrolysis, electric energy is converted into chemical energy.
   (d) A thermopile converts electric energy into heat energy.

10. A simple pendulum while passing through the mean position has:
    (a) minimum kinetic energy and maximum potential energy.
    (b) minimum potential energy and maximum kinetic energy.
    (c) minimum kinetic energy and minimum potential energy.
    (d) maximum kinetic energy and maximum potential energy.

11. Two water droplets coalesce to form a single drop. Then:
    (a) energy is released.
    (b) energy is absorbed
    (c) energy is dissipated
    (d) energy remains the same.

12. The work necessary to pull the body apart into its constituent particles is called the:
    (a) atomic energy          (b) binding energy
    (c) cohesive energy        (d) adhesive energy

13. A mechanical element for storing energy as a function of displacement is called:
    (a) gear                   (b) Atwood's machine
    (c) spring                 (d) capacitor

14. The sum total of the kinetic energy of the vibrating molecules is called:
    (a) heat energy
    (b) vibrational energy
    (c) molecular energy
    (d) mechanical equivalent of heat

15. Internal energy of a gas depends on:
    (a) pressure
    (b) volume
    (c) entropy
    (d) temperature

16. An example of converting light energy to electrical energy is:
    (a) thermocouple
    (b) photoelectric cell
    (c) electric lamp
    (d) action of light on a sensitised film

17. The gravitational potential energy of a particle with reference to earth:
    (a) increases with height.
    (b) decreases with height.
    (c) remains constant.
    (d) is always zero.

18. The direct conversion of energy into mass according to Einstein's equation, $E=mc^2$, is called:
    (a) materialisation
    (b) annihilation
    (c) pairing energy
    (d) pairing-exchange interaction

19. The production of nuclear energy is based on which formula?
    (a) $E=h\upsilon$
    (b) $H=U+pV$
    (c) $E=mc^2$
    (d) $w=fF.dl$

20. What is the form of energy that is transferred between two bodies due to difference in their temperatures?
    (a) radiation heat
    (b) heat
    (c) latent heat
    (d) specific heat

# 9

# CAUSE AND EFFECT

Nature is but a name for an effect Whose cause is God.

– WILLIAM COWPER

1. A body floating in a fluid displaces a weight of fluid equal to its own weight. This is known as:
   (a) Stokes' law
   (b) Torricelli's theorem
   (c) Archimedes' principle
   (d) Pascal's law

2. When an electric current passes round a circuit consisting of two dissimilar metals, heat is either absorbed or liberated at a junction. This is known as:
   (a) Peltier effect
   (b) Seebeck effect
   (c) Kelvin effect
   (d) Thomson effect

3. The direction of an induced electromotive force is always such as to oppose the cause that produces it. This is called:
   (a) Biot–Savert law
   (b) Lenz's law
   (c) Neumann's law
   (d) Faraday's third law of electromagnetic induction

4. The rate of cooling of a hot body is proportional to the mean excess of temperature of the hot body over the surroundings. This is known as:
   (a) First law of thermodynamics
   (b) Carnot–Clausius law
   (c) Joule's heating effect
   (d) Newton's law of cooling

5. The transmissibility of pressure is summarised in:
   (a) Archimedes' principle  (b) Bernoulli's theorem
   (c) Pascal's law           (d) Poiseuille's equation

6. At a constant temperature, the volume of a given mass of any gas is inversely proportional to the pressure upon the gas is called:
   (a) Gas law            (b) Mariotte's law
   (c) Charles' law       (d) Kelvin's law

7. Which of the following is not true about Boyle's law?
   (a) At high temperatures, Boyle's law is not obeyed.
   (b) Greater the pressure of a gas, smaller is the volume at a fixed temperature.
   (c) At very low temperatures, Boyle's law does not hold good.
   (d) The law is found to be only approximately true for real gases.

8. The edifice of classical mechanics was based upon:
   (a) Newton's law of gravitation
   (b) Newton's law of motion
   (c) Kepler's law of planetary motion
   (d) Einstein's theory of relativity

9. The change in apparent frequency of a source due to relative motion of source and observer is called:
   (a) Mossbauer effect     (b) Red shift
   (c) Hubble's law          (d) Doppler's effect

10. The liberation of heat by the passage of a current through an electric conductor due to its resistance is known as:
    (a) Joule's law           (b) Joule's effect
    (c) Joule–Kelvin effect   (d) Joule–Thomson effect

11. The emission of electrons from matter by electromagnetic radiation of certain energy is known as:
    (a) photoconductivity     (b) photovoltaic effect
    (c) photoelectric effect  (d) photoionisation

12. The recession velocity of a distant galaxy is in direct proportion to the distance from the observer. This is called:
    (a) Bode's law            (b) Doppler's effect
    (c) Red shift             (d) Hubble's law

13. Hydraulic brakes are based on:
    (a) pressure law
    (b) Pascal's law
    (c) Dulong and Petit's law
    (d) Dalton's law of partial pressure

14. Imagine yourself to be swimming in the wire in the direction of the current and facing a magnetic needle, then the north pole of the needle is deflected towards your left hand. Which is this rule?
    (a) Faraday's left hand rule  (b) Faraday's right hand rule
    (c) Ampère's rule             (d) Maxwell's rule

15. When a monochromatic light is passed through a transparent medium, some of the light is scattered. This scattering of light by molecules in which there is a change of frequency due to the molecules gaining or losing energy is summarised in the:
    (a) Compton effect          (b) Raman effect
    (c) Rayleigh scattering      (d) Tyndall effect

16. Name the model of the universe in which space–time began with an initial singularity (a point where the physical laws do not hold good) and subsequently expands?
    (a) Newtonian cosmology  (b) Pulsating theory
    (c) Steady State theory      (d) Big Bang theory

17. The most persuasive evidence that favours the Big Bang theory is the:
    (a) presence of the black holes in the universe.
    (b) birth and death stars.
    (c) existence of the cosmic microwave background radiations.
    (d) Hubble's law.

18. The law of equivalence of mass and energy is called:
    (a) law of conservation of mass
    (b) law of conservation of energy
    (c) Einstein's law
    (d) law of equivalent proportions

19. The path of ray in passing between two points during reflection or refraction is the path of lease time. This is summed up in:
    (a) Principle of least action  (b) Fermat's principle
    (c) Snell's law                  (d) Brewster's law

20. If the density of a substance is altered by some means, there is corresponding rise in the refractive index. This is called:
    (a) Kundt's rule
    (b) Snell's principle
    (c) Gladstone–Dale law
    (d) Hamilton's principle

# 10

# PHYSICAL PHENOMENA

Discovery consists of seeing what everybody has seen and thinking what nobody has thought.

– Albert Szent-Gyorgyi

1. The conversion of liquid into vapour at a temperature below the boiling point of the liquid is called:
   - (a) vaporisation
   - (b) condensation
   - (c) evaporation
   - (d) desiccation

2. Among the following, what is not true about evaporation?
   - (a) Evaporation takes place at all the temperatures.
   - (b) Evaporation produces cooling.
   - (c) Greater the surface area of the liquid, the quicker is the evaporation.
   - (d) Evaporation is nothing but boiling of the liquid at the highest temperature.

3. The rate of evaporation from a liquid can be increased if:
   - I.   the pressure above the liquid surface is increased.
   - II.  the temperature of the liquid is raised.
   - III. the area of the surface is increased.
   - IV.  a current of air passes over the liquid surface.

   Which combination is correct?
   - (a) I, II and III
   - (b) I, II and IV
   - (c) II, III and IV
   - (d) I, III and IV

4. Bending of light beams around the corner of an obstacle is called:
   (a) diffusion
   (b) diffraction
   (c) dispersion
   (d) deviation

5. When a beam of light strikes the surface of an optically less dense medium at an angle of incidence larger than the critical angle, it is reflected back into the optically denser medium. This phenomenon is called:
   (a) reflection
   (b) internal reflection
   (c) total internal reflection
   (d) total internal refraction

6. The scattering of a beam of light on reflection from a rough surface is called:
   (a) diffusion
   (b) dilation
   (c) dispersion
   (d) dissipation

7. The conversion of chemical energy into electrical energy in a cell is called:
   (a) electrification
   (b) discharge
   (c) transformation
   (d) decomposition

8. The decomposition of a beam of white light into its constituent colours is known as:
   (a) dispersion
   (b) dissemination
   (c) scattering
   (d) angular dispersion

9. Name the phenomenon in which a ray of light suffers change of direction when it enters another medium:
   (a) deviation
   (b) total internal reflection
   (c) dispersion
   (d) refraction

10. The process of forming ions is called:
    (a) ionisation
    (b) ionic conduction
    (c) ion migration
    (d) ion implantation

11. When a conductor is moved so that it cuts the magnetic flux linked with it, an electromotive force is induced between the ends of the conductor. This phenomenon is called:
    (a) electromagnetic interaction
    (b) electromagnetic induction
    (c) electrostatic induction
    (d) electromagnetic deflection

12. A process in which a nucleus emits particles either spontaneously or following a collision is called:
    (a) disintegration           (b) decomposition
    (c) transmutation            (d) electrodisintegration

13. If two tones of nearly the same frequencies are sounded together, the periodic waxing and waning of the resultant sound is called:
    (a) interference             (b) diffraction of sound
    (c) beat phenomenon          (d) coherence

14. The splitting of a heavy nucleus into fragments with the release of enormous energy is called:
    (a) nuclear fission          (b) nuclear disintegration
    (c) nuclear fusion           (d) thermonuclear reaction

15. Standing waves and echoes are based on which acoustic phenomenon?
    (a) interference             (b) polarisation
    (c) diffraction              (d) reflection

16. The formation of one element from another is called:
    (a) transmittancy            (b) transmittance
    (c) transmutation            (d) transmissivity

17. Ice-skating is possible because of the phenomenon of:
    (a) friction            (b) sublimation
    (c) relegation          (d) surface tension

18. The passage of the moon in front of a star or planet thus obscuring its light is called:
    (a) occultation         (b) eclipse
    (c) pericynthion        (d) apocynthion

19. The release of electrons from a solid as a result of its temperature is called:
    (a) photoemission       (b) thermionic emission
    (c) thermal emission    (d) electroemission

20. The persistence of audible sound after the source has been cut off is called:
    (a) echo                (b) resonance
    (c) acoustic prolongation  (d) reverberation

# 11

# KITH AND KIN OF PHYSICS

Science may set limits to knowledge, but should not set limits to imagination.

– BERTRAND RUSSELL

1. What is the science of sound?
   - (a) sonics
   - (b) eugenics
   - (c) acoustics
   - (d) phonics

2. What is the science of light and vision?
   - (a) photonics
   - (b) optics
   - (c) photochromics
   - (d) ophthalmology

3. What is the study of the phenomenon associated with electric charges at rest?
   - (a) frictional electricity
   - (b) electromagnetism
   - (c) electrodynamics
   - (d) electrostatics

4. The study of the forces on bodies and of the motion they produce is called:
   - (a) mechanics
   - (b) dynamics
   - (c) kinematics
   - (d) kinetics

5. What is the science concerned with the emission of electrons from hot bodies?
   (a) electronics
   (b) photonics
   (c) thermionics
   (d) solid state physics

6. What is the study of frequencies of about 20 kHz and upwards called?
   (a) sonics
   (b) supersonics
   (c) infrasonics
   (d) ultrasonics

7. The study of the interrelation between heat and other forms of energy is known as:
   (a) thermionics
   (b) thermodynamics
   (c) thermoelectricity
   (d) thermochemistry

8. Name the branch of Physics which deals with the calculation and measurement of light or of its time rate of flow:
   (a) photophysics
   (b) picosecond molecular process
   (c) photometry
   (d) photographic photometry

9. The study of the earth's atmosphere in its relation to weather and climate is known as:
   (a) meteorology
   (b) climatology
   (c) teratology
   (d) palaeoclimatology

10. The study of liquids at rest is called:
    (a) hydrology
    (b) hydrostatics
    (c) hydrometry
    (d) hydrophonics

11. What is the science of fluids in motion?
    (a) fluidics
    (b) fluid mechanics
    (c) fluid dynamics
    (d) hydraulics

12. What is the branch of Physics that deals with the dynamic properties of gases?
    (a) pneumatics          (b) aerodynamics
    (c) aerophysics          (d) aerology

13. The study of biological phenomena in terms of physical principles is called:
    (a) bionics              (b) biochemistry
    (c) biophysics           (d) bioengineering

14. What is the study of the physical properties of the earth?
    (a) earth science—geology (b) geophysics
    (c) palaeoecology        (d) palaeontology

15. What is the physical science of air?
    (a) avionics             (b) aeronautics
    (c) aerophysics          (d) aerology

16. What is the study of the processes governing the structure and development of clouds and release from them of precipitation?
    (a) meteorology          (b) climatology
    (c) weather science      (d) cloud physics

17. The study that deals with the application of modern physics to the problems of astronomy is called:
    (a) astronautics         (b) astrophysics
    (c) planetary physics    (d) cosmology

18. Cryogenics deals with the study of matter:
    (a) at low temperatures
    (b) at high temperatures
    (c) near absolute temperatures
    (d) near zero degree Celsius

19. What is the science of colours?
    (a) chromatics          (b) chromodynamics
    (c) chromatography     (d) chromolithography

20. The study of the origin and development of the universe is:
    (a) cosmology        (b) cosmogony
    (c) astrophysics      (d) teleology

# 12

# VIBRANT PHYSICS

The pendulum of the mind oscillates between sense and nonsense, not between right and wrong.

— Carl Gustav Jung

1. A sound wave passes from one medium to another. Which of the following parameters does not change?
   (a) amplitude          (b) frequency
   (c) wavelength       (d) velocity

2. The property of a wave which alters its surroundings is called:
   (a) interference        (b) noise
   (c) disturbance       (d) coherence

3. The maximum magnitude of the disturbance of a wave is known as:
   (a) amplitude         (b) displacement
   (c) distance          (d) wavelength

4. In the following diagram how many times is the wavelength greater than the amplitude of the wave?

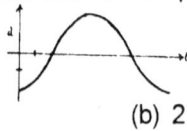

   (a) 1             (b) 2
   (c) 3             (d) 4

5. An acoustic wave caused by lightning is called:
   - (a) standing wave
   - (b) travelling wave
   - (c) thunder
   - (d) thunderstorm

6. In which of the following cases will the observed frequency of sound waves be greater than the actual frequency?
   - (a) When the source is moving away from a stationary object.
   - (b) When the observer is moving towards a stationary source of sound.
   - (c) When the observer is moving in the same direction as that of the source with the same speed.
   - (d) When the observer and the source are moving away from each other.

7. The waves in which the particles of the medium are displaced along the direction of propagation is called
   - (a) stationary wave
   - (b) progressive wave
   - (c) longitudinal wave
   - (d) transverse wave

(8) Which of the following statements is not true about X-rays?
   - (a) They can be deflected by a magnetic field.
   - (b) They exhibit the phenomenon of fluorescence.
   - (c) They cause photoelectric emission.
   - (d) They discharge electrified bodies.

9. Which of the following is not an electromagnetic radiation?
   - (a) light rays
   - (b) alpha rays
   - (c) gamma rays
   - (d) roentgen rays

10. The shorter the wavelength of light:
    (a) the smaller is the frequency.
    (b) the greater is the speed of light.
    (c) the easier it gets scattered.
    (d) the greater is its intensity.

11. The following figure shows a section of waves. The phenomenon suggests:

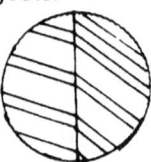

    (a) refraction            (b) diffraction
    (c) interference          (d) polarisation

12. RADAR makes the use of:
    (a) radiowaves of very long wavelengths.
    (b) radiowaves of very short wavelengths.
    (c) infrared waves of shorter wavelengths.
    (d) ultraviolet waves of longer wavelengths.

13. The compression waves of large amplitude arising from violent disturbances generated from a bomb blast are called:
    (a) stroke waves          (b) seismographic waves
    (c) shock waves           (d) standing waves

14. A light ray passes through a glass slab. Which of the following diagrams shows the correct path of the ray?

    (a)                       (b)

    (c)                       (d )

15. Among the following, what is the most important practical application of microwaves?
    (a) radar                    (b) TV
    (c) microwave oven           (d) radioastronomy

16. Which of the following diagrams depicts noises?

    (a) 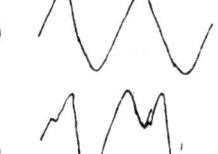    (b)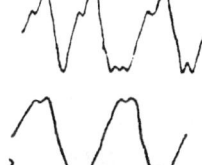

    (c)                          (d)

17. Which of the following electromagnetic radiations produces vitamins in the skin?
    (a) ultraviolet radiations
    (b) infrared radiations
    (c) microwave radiations
    (d) gamma radiations

18. The following figure depicts a part of the electromagnetic spectrum. 'C' is the region of visible light. Section 'A' represents the lowest frequency and Section 'E' the highest frequency. Which section depicts the infrared radiation?

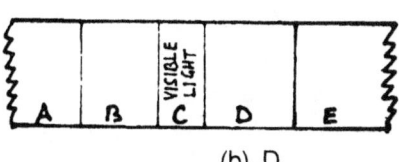

    (a) B                        (b) D
    (c) A                        (d) E

19. A white light OP passes through a prism, and its components get refracted, as shown in the following diagram The components A, B, C and D represent respectively:

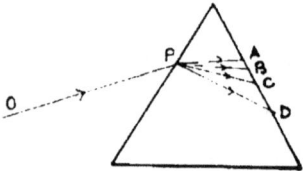

(a) blue, green, yellow, red
(b) green, yellow, blue, orange
(c) red, green, yellow, violet
(d) red, yellow, green, blue

20. What type of waves are produced by oscillation of free electrons?
    (a) radio waves        (b) infra-red rays
    (c) ultraviolet rays    (d) gamma rays

# 13

# PROPERTIES OF MATERIALS

For gold in physik is a cordial,
Therefore he lovede gold in special.
— GEOFFREY CHAUCER

1. The property of metals that allows them to be drawn
   into thin wires beyond their elastic limit without being
   ruptured is called:
   (a) ductility           (b) malleability
   (c) elasticity          (d) hardness

2. Interaction between the surfaces of two closely adjacent
   bodies which causes them to cling together is known
   as:
   (a) friction           (b) cohesion
   (c) adhesion         (d) viscosity

3. Solids which break above the elastic limit are called:
   (a) brittle            (b) ductile
   (c) plastic           (d) malleable

4. The property of some elementary particles that causes
   them to exert force on one another is known as:
   (a) potential difference     (b) charge
   (c) specific charge       (d) nucleon interaction

5. The property which permits the flow of current under the action of a potential difference is called:
   (a) resistance           (b) permeance
   (c) impedence            (d) conductance

6. When a body is resistant to heat, it is called:
   (a) thermoscopic         (b) thermotropic
   (c) thermoduric          (d) thermoplastic

7. The property of fluids by virtue of which they offer resistance to flow is known as:
   (a) gummosity            (b) glutinosity
   (c) viscidity            (d) viscosity

8. The tendency of a body to return to its original size or shape after having been deformed is called:
   (a) elastance            (b) elasticity
   (c) elastivity           (d) anelastivity

9. The emission of light by a material because of its high temperature is known as:
   (a) incandescence        (b) luminescence
   (c) scintillation        (d) phosphorescence

10. Which of the following statements is correct concerning the passage of white light into a glass prism?
   (a) The violet colour travels faster than the red colour.
   (b) The violet colour travels slower than the red colour.
   (c) All the colours of white light travel with the same speed.
   (d) Greater the wavelength, slower the speed of colour.

11. The property by virtue of which a body resists any attempt to change its state of rest or motion is called:
    (a) torpidity
    (b) passivity
    (c) inactivity
    (d) inertia

12. The property of an isolated conductor to store electric charge is:
    (a) capacitance
    (b) conductance
    (c) permeability
    (d) accumulation

13. If the properties of a body are the same in all directions, it is called:
    (a) isodynamic
    (b) isotropic
    (c) isogonic
    (d) isotopic

14. The property of an object that determines the direction of heat flow when in contact with another object is called:
    (a) calidity
    (b) pyrexia
    (c) caloric
    (d) temperature

15. The rate of flow of thermal energy through a material in the presence of a temperature gradient is called:
    (a) thermal capacity
    (b) thermal conductivity
    (c) thermal radiation
    (d) thermal convection

16. The property of some crystals of absorbing light to different extents, thereby giving to the crystals different colours according to the direction of the incident light is known as:
    (a) dichroism
    (b) dichromatism
    (c) diastrophism
    (d) chromaticity

17. Emission of radiations from a substance during illumination by radiations of higher frequency is called:
    (a) illuminance
    (b) fluorescence
    (c) radioluminescence
    (d) incandescence

18. If a material is feebly repelled by a magnet it is:
    (a) diamagnetic
    (b) paramagnetic
    (c) ferromagnetic
    (d) ferrimagnetic

19. The progressive decrease of a property as a result of repeated stress is called:
    (a) debility
    (b) rigidity
    (c) elastic deformation
    (d) fatigue

20. Property of some pure metals and their alloys at extremely low temperatures of having negligible resistance to the flow of an electric current is called:
    (a) supercharging
    (b) supercooling
    (c) superfluidity
    (d) superconductivity

# 14

# MICROCOSMOS

Man is slightly nearer to the atom than the stars. From his central position he can survey the grandest works of Nature with the astronomer, or the minutest works with the physicists
— ARTHUR EDDINGTON

1. Name the light and stable fundamental particle which carries a negative electric charge:
   (a) electron          (b) positron
   (c) neutrino          (d) neutron

2. What is the anti-particle of an electron?
   (a) negatron          (b) negaton
   (c) negative electron (b) positron

3. The quantum of electromagnetic radiation is called:
   (a) phonon            (b) photon
   (c) pion              (d) quanta

4. An ion is an electrically charged:
   (a) atom
   (b) molecule
   (c) group of atoms or group of molecules
   (d) any of the above

5. What is the charge conjugate of a proton?
   (a) electron           (b) neutron
   (c) antiproton         (d) meson

6. What is an alpha particle?
   (a) A fast moving proton
   (b) The nucleus of deuterium
   (c) The nucleus of hydrogen atom
   (d) The nucleus of helium atom

7. The elements that have the same number of protons but different masses are known as:
   (a) isotopes           (b) isobars
   (c) isotones           (d) isomers

8. Thermions are:
   (a) electrons          (b) photons
   (c) mesons             (d) protons

9. Which among the following is not true about the nucleus of an atom?
   (a) It holds about 99.9% of the atomic mass.
   (b) It is the exclusive habitat of only protons and neutrons.
   (c) It is the source of radioactivity.
   (d) Like atom, it can also be fragmented.

10. Which is the lightest isotope?
    (a) protium           (b) deuterium
    (c) tritium           (d) none of them

11. What is the most abundant element in the universe?
    (a) hydrogen          (b) helium
    (c) carbon            (d) oxygen

12. When a stream of alpha particles is sent through a thin metal foil, most of the particles penetrate the foil because:
    (a) they move with very high velocities.
    (b) they are positively charged.
    (c) they are very penetrating.
    (d) the bulk of the atom consists of empty space.

13. What constitute gamma rays?
    (a) Fast moving photons
    (b) Fast moving positrons
    (c) Electromagnetic radiation
    (d) Streams of neutrinos

14. Tritium is:
    I.   the heaviest isotope of hydrogen.
    II.  the only isotope of hydrogen that is radioactive.
    III. present in natural hydrogen in the ratio of one atom to $10^{17}$ atoms.

    Which of the following combinations is correct?
    (a) I and II only          (b) I and III only
    (c) II and III only        (d) I, II and III

15. What is not true about photon?
    (a) Its rest mass is zero.
    (b) It travels with the speed of light.
    (c) Its energy is entirely kinetic.
    (d) It has a momentum equal to $h\lambda$.

16. The sum of the masses of constituent particles of a nucleus of atom is:
    (a) greater than the mass of the nucleus.
    (b) smaller than the mass of the nucleus.
    (c) equal to the mass of the nucleus.
    (d) always varying.

17. Name the hypothetical particle that moves faster than light?
    (a) graviton      (b) chronon
    (c) tachyon      (d) tauon

18. The ion that has lost one or more electrons and has a net positive charge is:
    (a) anion      (b) cation
    (c) metallic ion      (d) gaseous ion

19. A 'sound' quantum is termed as:
    (a) chronon      (b) tachyon
    (c) accauston      (d) phonon

20. A fundamental particle of which 'elementary particles' are believed to be composed of is termed as:
    (a) glucon      (b) graviton
    (c) quark      (d) lepton

# 15

## MACROCOSMOS

Not only is the universe stranger than we imagine, it is stranger that we can imagine.

— ARTHUR EDDINGTON

1. Name the planet where its day is longer than its year:
   (a) Pluto
   (b) Neptune
   (c) Venus
   (d) Jupiter

2. Which of the following pair of planets has no natural satellite?
   (a) Venus and Pluto
   (b) Venus and Mercury
   (c) Venus and Mars
   (d) Mercury and Pluto

3. Which is the only natural satellite in the solar system that has a dense atmosphere?
   (a) Titan
   (b) Triton
   (c) Callisto
   (d) Ganymede

4. Who discovered Titan, a natural satellite of Saturn and the biggest satellite in the solar system?
   (a) Tycho Brahe
   (b) Johannes Kepler
   (c) Galileo Galeli
   (d) Christiaan Huygens

5. Which planet is known as 'red planet'?
   (a) Mars　　　　　　　(b) Jupiter
   (c) Neptune　　　　　 (d) Saturn

6. What is the foremost speciality of these heavenly bodies:
   Io, Ganymede, Callisto, and Europa?
   I.　These are natural satellites of the planet Jupiter.
   II.　All these satellites are the four biggest satellites of
   Jupiter.
   III. All these satellites of Jupiter were discovered by
   Galileo.

   Which of the following combinatious is correct?
   (a) I only　　　　　　 (b) I and II only
   (c) I, II and III　　　　(d) none of these

7. Which is the most widely known and oldest of the
   constellations?
   (a) Ursa Minor　　　　(b) Ursa Major
   (c) Taurus　　　　　　(d) Gemini

8. A cool star having a large diameter and high luminosity
   is called:
   (a) white dwarf　　　　(b) neutron star
   (c) red giant　　　　　(d) black hole

9. Remnant of the core of a star that has exhausted its
   nuclear fuel is known as:
   (a) white dwarf　　　　(b) nova
   (c) supernova　　　　 (d) interstellar gases

10. A non-terrestrial body which survives passage through
    the earth's atmosphere and arrives as a solid at the
    surface of the earth is called:
    (a) astroid　　　　　　(b) meteor
    (c) micro-meteorite　　(d) meteorite

11. A hypothetical enclosure of infinite radius with its centre at the observer is known as:
    (a) nadir
    (b) zenith
    (c) celestial sphere
    (d) celestial equator

12. A rare and violent class of stellar flare-up is:
    (a) nova
    (b) supernova
    (c) novae stellae
    (d) nebule

13. Which is the brightest star visible from earth?
    (a) Vega
    (b) Antares
    (c) Sirius
    (d) Rigel

14. Galaxies are grouped according to their shapes: spiral, elliptical, and irregular. Who classified the galaxies for the first time?
    (a) Edwin Hubble
    (b) Sir John Frederick Herschel
    (c) Sir William Herschel
    (d) S. Chandrasekhar

15. Which is the second closest star to sun?
    (a) Epsilon Eridani
    (b) Bernard Star
    (c) 61 Cygni
    (d) Kappa Pavonis

16. A faint star that undergoes explosion during which its luminosity increases up to one hundred thousand times is called:
    (a) globular cluster
    (b) nebule
    (c) nova
    (d) supernova

17. This photograph shows an extremely hot thin outer envelope of gas around the sun. This is termed as:

  (a) photosphere          (b) solar flare
  (c) solar prominence     (d) corona

18. The dark areas on the sun produced by the most intense magnetic fields are called:
  (a) sundog             (b) sun spots
  (c) plages             (d) prominences

19. The astronomical scale of brightness of stars and planet is called:
  (a) magnitude         (b) absolute magnitude
  (c) apparent magnitude   (d) visible magnitude

20. A star that cannot generate thermonuclear energy is called:
  (a) dwarf star         (b) carbon star
  (c) black dwarf        (d) dead star

## 16

## LOGICAL PHYSICS

Logical consequences are the scarecrows of fools and the beacons of wise men.

– T.H. HUXLEY

1. Among the following pendulums, whose time period is greatest?

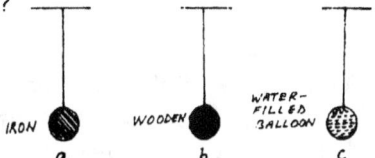

   (a) iron pendulum        (b) wooden pendulum
   (b) water-filled ballon    (d) same for all

2. You are equipped with a very powerful earphone to listen to a hydrogen bomb explosion on the surface of the moon. The shockwave moves at a velocity of 'v' m/s. The distance between the earth and moon is 'd'.

   When do you expect to hear the sound?
   (a) Immediately after explosion
   (b) Never
   (c) After d/v seconds
   (d) After v/d seconds

3. A coloured piece of glass bangle is between two plane mirrors which are inclined to each other at different angles as shown in the diagram.

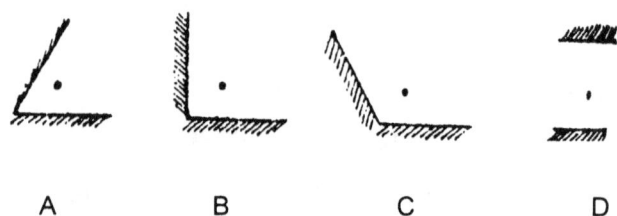

| A | B | C | D |

In which case the number of images is maximum?
(a) A                                    (b) B
(c) C                                    (d) D

4. Ball 'A', moving with certain velocity, strikes another ball 'B' which is at rest. Ball 'B' is four times heavier than ball 'A'. After collision, ball 'B' starts moving in the forward direction with half the velocity of the initial velocity of ball 'A'.

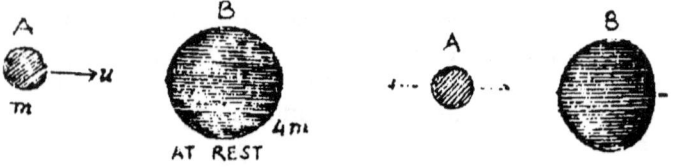

Ball 'A', after collision, will move with the same velocity
(a) as before, but in forward direction.
(b) as before, but in backward direction.
(c) as that of ball 'B', but in forward direction.
(d) as that of ball 'B' but in backward direction.

5. Two spherical balls 'A' and 'B' are moving with the same kinetic energy. Mass of ball 'B' is four times the mass of ball 'A'.

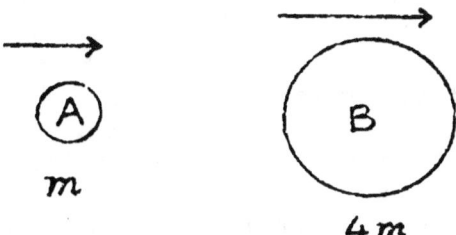

What will be the momentum of ball 'B'?
(a) one-fourth of ball 'A'      (b) one-half of ball 'A'
(c) twice that of ball 'A'      (d) four times that of ball 'A'

6. The upper-half of a convex lens is covered by a black paper, as shown in the diagram below:

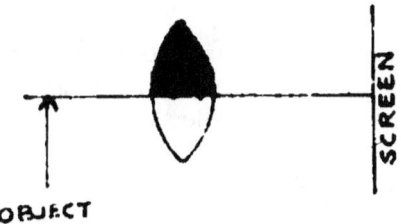

Which of the following statements is correct?
(a) A complete image is formed on the screen but with decreased intensity.
(b) The upper-half of the image is disappeared.
(c) The lower-half of the image is disappeared.
(d) Only the lower-half of the image is formed, but with increased intensity.

7. Following figures appear on an oscillograph:

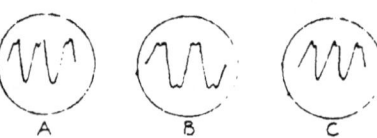

Which represents noise?
(a) A and B
(b) A and C
(c) all the three
(d) none of these

8. Which among the following is correct when a bullet is fired from a rifle?
(a) The bullet has less kinetic energy but more speed.
(b) The bullet has less kinetic energy but greater momentum.
(c) The bullet has greater kinetic energy and greater momentum.
(d) The bullet has more kinetic energy, but momenta of bullet and rifle are equal.

9. Two cylinders – one hollow and the other solid – having the same mass and same diameter are allowed to roll down from an inclined plane. Which reaches the bottom first?
(a) hollow cylinder
(b) solid cylinder
(c) both reach at the same time
(d) the one having higher density reaches earlier

10. A car is moving with a certain speed. Suddenly, it is accelerated in such a manner that its momentum is doubled. Its kinetic energy will become:
(a) half
(b) two times
(c) four times
(d) eight times

11. In which of the following cases the amount of work done is most?

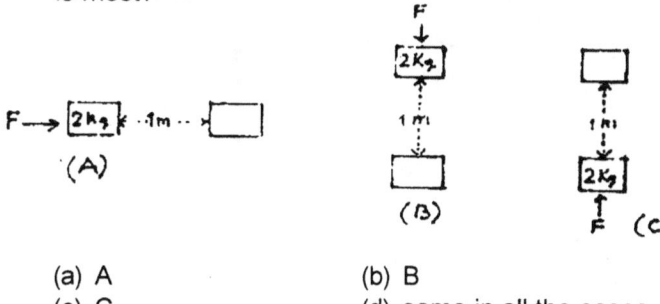

(a) A
(b) B
(c) C
(d) same in all the cases

12. A Maruti car and a DTC bus, moving with the same kinetic energy, are brought to rest by applying brakes which provide the same retarding force. Which comes to rest in shorter distance?
(a) DTC bus
(b) Maruti car
(c) The one moving with greater speed.
(d) Both come to rest after travelling the same distance.

13. At what angle should two equal forces exert on a particle simultaneously so that the resultant force is equal to either of the two forces?
(a) 60°
(b) 90°
(c) 120°
(d) 180°

14. The image of an object is found to be virtual, erect, and diminished. The object is in front of a:
(a) convex lens and very far from it.
(b) convex lens and very close to it.
(c) convex mirror and very close to it.
(d) concave mirror and very close to it.

15. You are moving towards a stationary plane mirror at the speed of light 'c'. Your image will move towards you at a speed of:

MIRROR

(a) c
(b) 2c
(c) $\sqrt{c}$
(d) c/2

16. A stream of water flows through a tube of varying diameter as shown in the diagram:

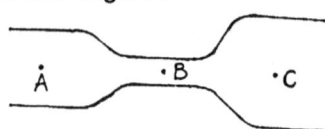

At what point its velocity is maximum?
(a) A
(b) B
(c) C
(d) same at every point

17. Two cylinders – 'A' and 'B' – of equal capacities are filled in with two different gases having same pressure at the same temperature. Now, the gases from both the cylinders are allowed to be mixed in cylinder 'C' of the same capacity at the same temperature.

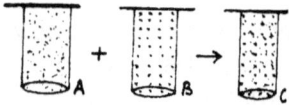

The pressure of the mixed gas in cylinder 'C' will be:
(a) halved
(b) doubled
(c) quadrupled
(d) the same

18. The refractive index of glass with respect to air is 3/2 and that of water with respect to air is 4/3. What is the refractive index of glass with respect to water?
    (a) 2:1                          (b) 1:2
    (c) 9:8                          (d) 8:9

19. The focal length of an equi-convex lens is 'f'. If it is cut along its axis MN, what will be the focal length of each half?

    (a) f/2                          (b) f
    (c) 2f                           (d) 2/f

20. Four copper cylinders A, B, C, and D have different lengths and diameters as shown in the following diagrams ('L' represents length and 'D' the diameter.)

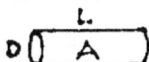    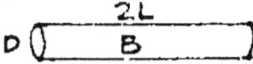

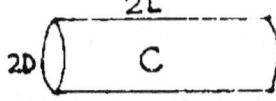    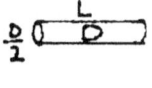

    Which cylinder has the smallest electrical resistance?
    (a) A                            (b) B
    (c) C                            (d) D

# 17

# MAKERS OF PHYSICS

We have found a strange footprint on the shores of the unknown. We have devised profound theories, one after another, to account for its origins. At last we have succeeded in reconstructing the creature that made the footprint. And lo! It is our own.

– ARTHUR EDDINGTON

1. Name the great pre-Christian era Greek mathematician who established the basic theory of gravity and the principle of the lever, besides his outstanding contributions in hydrostatics.
   (a) Pythagoras         (b) Archimedes
   (c) Aristotle            (d) Socrates

2. Who was the first physicist to measure the gravitational constant G with a torsion balance and thus calculating the mean density of the earth?
   (a) Sir Isaac Newton     (b) N. Maskelyne
   (c) Charles Coulomb     (d) Henry Cavendish

3. Name the book-binder, and later assistant to Sir Humphry Davy, who was responsible for devising an electric motor in 1831:
   (a) Joseph Henry       (b) Michael Faraday
   (c) Heinrich Lenz       (d) William Whewell

4. He introduced the terms 'positive' and 'negative' as used in electricity, and was most famous for his research on lightning and establishing the electrical nature of the discharge. Who was he?
   (a) William Gilbert     (b) Jean Baptiste Perrin
   (b) Sir John Franklin    (d) Benjamin Franklin

5. He was a pioneer in the study of springs. He discovered a fundamental law in elasticity, besides inventing the conical pendulum. Who was this contemporary of Newton?
   (a) John Harrison
   (b) Robert Hooke
   (c) Anthony van Leeuwenhoek
   (d) Christiaan Huygens

6. Who invented a code, bearing his name, in which dots and dashes represent alphabets for the purpose of telegraphic communications?
   (a) Sir Oliver Joseph Lodge  (b) W.J. Cooke
   (c) Charles Wheatstone    (d) Samuel Morse

7. Besides inventing a hydrometer that bears his name, he was the first physicist in England to decompose water by electrolysis through his self-devised voltaic pile. Who was he?
   (a) John Daniell     (b) Alessandro Volta
   (c) William Nicholson  (d) Henri Regnault

8. Who invented the hygrometer, but was otherwise more famous for his simple cell?
   (a) Georges Leclanche  (b) William Nicholson
   (c) John Daniell      (d) Gustav Fechner

9. Name the wealthy physicist who made investigations to detect motion of the hypothetical medium ether, measured the velocity of light, besides devising a method to determine the coefficient of expansion of small crystals.
   - (a) Armand Fizeau
   - (b) Augustin Fresnel
   - (c) Albert Michelson
   - (d) Edward Morley

10. He determined the law of the flow of electricity and also established rules for cells in series and parallel. Who was this physicist whose name is also associated with a unit in electrical measurement?
    - (a) James Watt
    - (b) George Simon Ohm
    - (c) Alessandro Volta
    - (d) André Ampère

11. Though he graduated in arts and theology, he was a prolific science writer. His main field of research was diffraction of light, but he is more famous for the invention of the kaleidoscope, which he made in 1816. Who was he?
    - (a) Sir David Brewster
    - (b) Sir William Hamilton
    - (c) Jules Jamin
    - (d) Thomas Young

12. Among the following, who was a pioneer in the field of vacuum discharge tube, apart from discovering the element thallium?
    - (a) Henry Geissler
    - (b) William Crookes
    - (c) Michael Faraday
    - (d) Wilhelm Roentgen

13. Who invented the thermionic valves?
    - (a) Lee de Forest
    - (b) Owen Richardson
    - (c) John Fleming
    - (d) Philipp Lenard

14. The inventor of the first scale of temperature, Anders Celsius was basically:
    (a) an astronomer          (b) a chemist
    (c) a palaeographist        (d) a palaeontologist

15. Physician by profession, this great scientist made advances in the field of magnetism and electrostatics, introduced the terms 'electricity', 'electric force', 'magnetic pole', etc. Who was this sixteenth century scientist?
    (a) Gottfried Leibnitz      (b) Josiah Gibbs
    (c) William Gilbert         (d) Hans Christian Oersted

16. This handsome seventeen-year-old boy later became one of the greatest scientists of all times. Whose photograph is this?

    (a) Albert Einstein         (b) Max Planck
    (c) Ernest Rutherford       (d) Prince Louis de Broglie

17. For over forty years he carried out experiments to establish the relationship between heat and mechanical energy, besides his investigations on the heating effects of electric current. Who was this physicist in whose name the unit of energy is assigned?
    (a) Henry Rowland           (b) James Prescott Joule
    (c) Heinrich Lenz           (d) J.R. von Mayer

18. At the age of twenty-two, he took out the first wireless telegraph patent, and shared the Nobel Prize for Physics in 1909. Who was this supporter of Mussolini?
    (a) Sir Oliver Joseph Lodge
    (b) Sir Jagadish Chandra Bose
    (c) Sir Charles Wheatstone
    (d) Guglielmo Marconi

19. Name the French physicist who established the relationship between pressure and volume of a gas known as Boyle's law outside France?
    (a) Edmé Mariotté            (b) Henri Moissan
    (c) Jacques Charles          (d) Jean Baptiste Perrin

20. Who was the inventor of the pressure cooker?
    (a) James Watt               (b) Charles Parsons
    (c) Denis Papin              (d) Henry Rowland

**18**

# REASONING IN PHYSICS

If a man will begin with certainties, he shall end in doubts, but if he will be content to begin with doubts, he shall end in certainties.

– Francis Bacon

1. Why does the word 'TOXOT' looks exactly as it is when viewed through a plane mirror? Because:
   (a) TOXOT is an anagram.
   (b) TOXOT is a palindrome.
   (c) TOXOT is laterally inverted.
   (d) The image of TOXOT is virtual.

2. A fielder lowers his hands backwards while holding a catch because:
   (a) the force decreases as time increases.
   (b) the velocity decreases with time.
   (c) the momentum decreases with time.
   (d) it is a style of holding a catch.

3. Though steam and boiling water are at the same temperature, yet steam causes more severe burn, because:
   (a) kinetic energy is more in steam.
   (b) steam is in gaseous form.
   (c) steam possesses latent heat.
   (d) energy is dissipated in boiling water but not in steam.

4. A chain of hydrogen bombs is being exploded every time in the sun due to the fusion process, yet you do not hear the sound, because:
   (a) the sun is very far away.
   (b) the sound so generated dissipates away.
   (c) the sound so generated is absorbed by various layers of the sun.
   (d) the space between the sun and the earth is void.

5. Motorists use a convex mirror in their vehicles because:
   (a) it gives an erect image of the object.
   (b) it gives an erect and wider view.
   (c) It gives an erect and diminished view.
   (d) It gives a diminished and wider view.

6. Why does the sun generally appear to be red at sunset?
   (a) The atmosphere scatters light of shorter wavelengths more effectively than the light of longer wavelengths.
   (b) The atmosphere scatters light of longer wavelengths more effectively than the light of shorter wavelengths.
   (c) This is due to the total internal reflection.
   (d) This is because the temperature falls in the evenings.

7. Why do diamonds sparkle?
   (a) When a light beam enters a diamond it suffers multiple refraction, thus making it brilliant.
   (b) Since diamond has many faces, light falling on it scatters, and hence it shines.
   (c) When light enters the diamond, it suffers total internal reflection again and again, thus making each face shine.
   (d) Since a diamond has many faces that are cut in irregular fashion, there is a constant phase difference between the incident and refracted light, which makes a diamond shine.

8. An astronaut feels weightlessness inside an artificial satellite, because:
   (a) at that altitude the acceleration due to gravity is zero.
   (b) the total mechanical energy of the satellite is negative.
   (c) the satellite is in circular orbit, so due to centripetal force the astronaut feels so.
   (d) he experiences no force.

9. The sky is blue due to:
   (a) the reflection of the white light by dust particles.
   (b) the refraction of white light by the atmosphere.
   (c) scattering of white light by dust particles and molecules of air.
   (d) scattering of white light by the oceans.

10. Mud huts are cooler in summer and warmer in winter because:
   (a) the main material of mud huts, i.e. clay is a poor conductor of heat.
   (b) mud huts are compact and do not allow the heat inside to escape easily.
   (c) the top of mud huts is usually dry grass which absorb the external heat.
   (d) there are not many openings in the huts, as such heat does not escape.

11. Why does a glass tumbler containing ice-cool drink show droplets of water on its outer surface?
   (a) Tiny holes between the glass molecules help the liquid to ooze out.
   (b) This is due to the difference of temperatures between inside and outside of the glass.
   (c) Water vapours present in the atmosphere condense to form dews on it.
   (d) Difference in temperatures between ice-cool drink and air outside glass increases the relative humidity.

12. Depression on sand is more when you are standing than when you are lying down, because:
    (a) thrust is more in standing position.
    (b) in lying position, more area is involved so thrust is less and pressure is more.
    (c) in standing position, for equal thrust, area is smaller so pressure is more.
    (d) centre of gravity lowers down while lying down, so pressure is more.

13. Why two blocks of ice when put together and compressed become a single block of ice?
    (a) Melting point of ice decreases when pressure is increased.
    (b) Melting point of ice increases when pressure is increased.
    (c) Ice blocks attract each other to form a bond.
    (d) Latent heat of fusion of ice is high.

14. The light of a torch becomes dim when it is put on for a longer period. Why?
    (a) When the current from dry cells is continuously drawn, polarisation sets in and the current becomes weaker.
    (b) Since the dry cells are in series, the total internal resistance of dry cells increases when in continuous use, and thus the current becomes weaker.
    (c) The electrolyte of dry cells gets decomposed if current flows for longer time in one stretch.
    (d) Flow of electrons is retarded by the electrolyte of dry cells due to local action and hence the current diminishes.

15. A long jumper runs faster before taking a leap in order to gain:
    - (a) energy
    - (b) power
    - (c) force
    - (d) momentum

16. An empty vessel produces louder sound than a filled one because:
    - (a) the density of air is less than the density of liquid contained in the vessel when filled.
    - (b) the air molecules in empty vessel have greater amplitude and hence greater intensity than liquid molecules in the filled vessel.
    - (c) the liquid in the filled vessel absorbs the vibrations of the liquid molecules.
    - (d) the kinetic energy of particles constituting the air column is greater as compared to the kinetic energy of particles of liquid column.

17. Why does a balloon stop rising when it attains a certain height?
    - (a) The balloon will stop rising when the upthrust on it becomes equal to its weight.
    - (b) At a particular height, the net gravitational force on the balloon is zero, and hence it remains balanced.
    - (c) The air pressure diminishes with height and hence at a particular height the equilibrium is reached.
    - (d) At a certain height the pressure inside the balloon is in equilibrium with the pressure outside it.

18. White clothes are preferred in summer because white bodies are:
    - (a) good reflectors and poor absorbers.
    - (b) poor absorbers and poor emitters.
    - (c) poor absorbers and poor transmitters.
    - (d) good emitters and poor transmitters.

19. Birds do not feel electric shock while sitting on current-carrying uninsulated wires because:
    (a) the feathers of birds act as an insulator and hence the current does not pass through them.
    (b) the resistance offered by the body of birds is very high.
    (c) the current does not pass through the body as the claws of birds are non-conducting.
    (d) the potential difference between the two claws of birds is very small.

20. During severe winters when lakes are frozen, fishes still survive. Why?
    (a) The fishes can withstand very low temperatures.
    (b) The bottom of the lake is not frozen.
    (c) The ice acts as an insulator and thus prevents low thermal currents to reach the bottom.
    (d) The fishes remain in the state of hibernation.

# 19

# EXPERIMENTAL PHYSICS

A scientist in his laboratory is not only a technician, he is also a child placed before natural phenomena which impress him like a fairy tale.

– MARIE CURIE

1. In 1798, Henry Cavendish performed a classic experiment, known as 'Cavendish experiment'. It was aimed at:
   (a) studying the composition of the atmosphere.
   (b) establishing the relation between heat and energy.
   (c) investigating the law of force between electrical charges.
   (d) measuring Newton's gravitational constant.

2. Which of the following devices does not demonstrate the interference of light?
   (a) Quincke's tube
   (b) Young's double slit
   (c) Lloyd's mirror
   (d) Fresnel's bi-prism

3. The 1847 Joule's experiment was aimed at:
   (a) investigating the heating effect of electric current.
   (b) determining the temperature for the maximum density of water.
   (c) determining the mechanical equivalent of heat.
   (d) investigating the internal energy of gas.

4. For comparing the thermal conductivity of a good conductor, which of the following devices is employed?
   (a) Searl's method
   (b) Ingen–Hausz's apparatus
   (c) Jaeger and Diesselhorst's method
   (d) Gregory and Archer's method

5. Kundt's tube may be used to:
   I.   determine the velocity of sound in a gas.
   II.  compare the velocity of sound in a gas and in a solid.
   III. compare the velocity of sound in two different gases.
   IV. determine the ratio of the specific heats of a gas.

   Which combination is true?
   (a) I and III only
   (b) I, II and III only
   (c) I, II, III and IV
   (d) I, II and IV

6. A resonance tube apparatus is employed to:
   (a) study beats.
   (b) verify the laws of vibrating strings.
   (c) investigate the dependence of velocity of sound in air upon temperature.
   (d) determine the velocity of sound in air.

7. A potentiometer may be employed for:
   I. comparing the e.m.f.s of two primary cells.
   II. comparing two small resistances.
   III. studying the variation in potential drop with the length of wire.
   IV. determining the internal resistance of a primary cell.

   Which combination is correct?
   (a) I, II and III
   (b) I, II and IV
   (c) II, III and IV
   (d) I, II, III and IV

8. What happens to an electron beam when a uniform magnetic field is applied at right angles to it?
   (a) The beam starts oscillating.
   (b) The beam is deflected in a parabolic path.
   (c) The beam is deflected in a circular path.
   (d) The beam remains unaffected.

9. In Millikan's famous oil-drop method for determining the harge on an electron, the experimental measurements show that the oil-drops gain whole or integral number of charges because:
   (a) the oil-drop falls with a terminal velocity.
   (b) the oil-drop is never stationary.
   (c) the charges are multiples of the smallest charge.
   (d) the oil-drop is circular.

10. In a cathode ray oscillograph, the electron beam is focused by varying:
    (a) the anode potential.
    (b) the grid voltage.
    (c) the screen potential.
    (d) the time-base voltage.

11. In 1902, who among the following conducted an important experiment to infer that the rate of electron-emission depends only on its temperature?
    (a) J.A. Flemings
    (b) O.W. Richardson
    (c) Lee de Forest
    (d) T.A. Edison

12. Einstein's most famous equation, $E=mc^2$, whereby mass of a body and energy are interconvertible, may be experimentally verified by:
    I.   explosion of atomic bomb
    II.  cosmic ray showers
    III. nuclear transformations

    Which of the following combinations is correct?
    (a) I and II only         (b) I and III only
    (c) II and III only       (d) I, II and III

13. In August 1912, Vector Hess performed a very important experiment by sending a hydrogen-filled balloon along with an ionisation counter to the upper atmosphere. The counter recorded that the rate of ionisation is directly proportional to the height of the balloon. This led to the discovery of:
    (a) electromagnetic radiations
    (b) cosmic rays
    (c) neutrinos
    (d) mesons

14. The first purely artificial nuclear disintegration was experimentally carried out by:
    (a) Prof E.O. Lawrence     (b) Enrico Fermi
    (c) Cockcroft and Walton    (d) Robert van de Graaff

15. Who was the first experimentalist to determine the velocity of light by purely terrestrial observations?
    (a) Forbes
    (b) Young
    (c) Cornu
    (d) Fizeau

16. The main conclusion drawn from Rutherford's experiment on the scattering of alpha particles was that:
    (a) alpha particles are positively charged.
    (b) the positive charges inside an atom are uniformly distributed.
    (c) the positive charges inside the atom are concentrated at the core of the atom.
    (d) the atom is neutral.

17. Rutherford was the first physicist to carry artificial transmutation from one element into another. In his experiment he bombarded nitrogen with alpha particles to produce isotope of:
    (a) oxygen
    (b) carbon
    (c) hydrogen
    (d) helium

18. Henry Becquerel discovered radioactivity in 1896. Soon after Rutherford investigated the penetrating power of the radiations from uranium and identified two types of rays which he called alpha and beta rays. Who, of the following, later discovered the third kind of radiations, which were called gamma rays?
    (a) Madam Curie
    (b) Soddy
    (c) Villard
    (d) Fajans

19. Electron microscope uses beam instead of light rays. It is based on which of the two principles?
    I.   Particle nature of electrons.
    II.  Wave nature of electrons.
    III. Electrons can be focused by electric and magnetic fields.
    IV.  Electrons carry negative charges.

    Which of the following combinations is correct?
    (a) I and III                     (b) III and IV
    (c) II and III                    (d) II and IV

20. Which of the following International Awards is given annually for distinguished current work in experimental physics?
    (a) Thomas Young Prize
    (b) Paul Dirac Prize
    (c) Charles Chree Prize
    (d) Charles Vernon Boys Prize

# 20

# NOBEL PHYSICS

The true men of action in our time, those who transform the world, are not the politicians and statesmen, but the scientists.
– W.H. Auden

1. Expelled from school, he couldn't go to the university, but had the distinction of being the first recipient of the Noble Prize in Physics. Who was he?
   (a) Emil von Behring
   (b) Jacobus Vant Hoff
   (c) Wilhelm Conrad Roentgen
   (d) Hendrik Antoon Lorentz

2. The first husband–wife team to get the Nobel Prize for for Physics was:
   (a) Carl Cori–Getty Cori
   (b) Pierre Curie–Marie Curie
   (c) Frederick Joliot–Irene Jolio-Curie
   (d) Gunnar Myrdal–Alva Myrdal

3. Who is the only person to have ever received the Nobel Prize for Physics twice?
   (a) John Bardeen          (b) Linus Pauling
   (c) Marie Curie           (d) Frederick Sanger

4. At the age of twenty-five who was the youngest person ever to have received the Nobel Prize for Physics?
   (a) Paul Dirac
   (b) William Lawrence Bragg
   (c) Tsung Dao Lee
   (d) Werner Karl Heisenberg

5. He was barely eighteen when he had an original research paper on optics published. He earned the first Nobel Prize in science for his country and also earned the knighthood one year before the Nobel Prize for Physics. Who was he?
   (a) Sir Edward Appleton
   (b) Sir John Douglas Cockcroft
   (c) Sir William Bragg
   (d) Sir C.V. Raman

6. Who was the first Asian to win the Nobel Prize for Physics?
   (a) Sir C.V. Raman       (b) Hideki Yukawa
   (c) Sin-Itiro Tomonaga   (d) Leo Esaki

7. Antoine Henri Becquerel was awarded the Nobel Prize in 1903 for:
   (a) demonstrating the influence of earth's magnetic field on its atmosphere.
   (b) diffraction of X-rays.
   (c) discovering spontaneous radioactivity.
   (d) investigating the absorption of light by crystal.

8. Who shared the 1983 Nobel Prize for Physics with William Fowler for their research on processes involved in stellar evolution?
   (a) Hans Bethe
   (b) Subrahmanyam Chandrasekhar
   (c) Polykarp Kusch
   (d) Kenneth Wilson

9. Which is the only father–son team that has ever shared the Nobel Prize for Physics?
   (a) J.J. Thomson–G.P. Thomson
   (b) Hans von Euler–Ulf von Euler
   (c) Niels Bohr–Aage Bohr
   (d) W.H. Bragg–W.L. Bragg

10. Carl Anderson, the discoverer of positron, was just thirty-one when he received the Nobel Prize for Physics. Who among the following got the Prize at the same age?
   (a) P.A.M. Dirac
   (b) W.K. Heisenberg
   (c) T.D. Lee
   (d) all the above

11. Who, among the following was the oldest person at the time of receiving the Nobel Prize for Physics?
   (a) Peter Kapitza
   (b) S. Chandrasekhar
   (c) Heike Kamerlingh-Onnes
   (d) Nicolaas Bloembergen

12. For which work was Albert Einstein awarded the Nobel Prize?
   (a) Special theory of relativity
   (b) General theory of relativity
   (c) Discovery of photoelectric effect
   (d) Brownian motion

13. With whom did Guglielmo Marconi share the Nobel Prize in 1909 for developing wireless telegraphy?
   (a) Owen Richardson
   (b) Ludwig Gustav Hertz
   (c) Sir Jagadish Chandra Bose
   (d) Carl Ferninand Braun

14. Who was awarded the Nobel Prize for the discovery of the first known particle of anti-matter?
    (a) Carl David Anderson
    (b) Philip Anderson
    (c) Sherwood Anderson
    (d) Elizabeth Garrett Anderson

15. Lord Rayleigh was the first Englishman to win the Nobel Prize for Physics in 1904 for his discovery of argon. What was his real name?
    (a) William Ramsay          (b) Charles Wilson
    (c) William Thomson         (d) John William Strutt

16. Who was awarded the Nobel Prize for Physics for discovering the wave nature of particles?
    (a) Owen Richardson         (b) Louis de Broglie
    (c) Erwin Schrödinger       (d) Isodor Isaac Rabi

17. One of the most remarkable breakthroughs in Physics was the principle leading to the discovery of the transistor, and for this the 1956 Nobel Prize was awarded to:
    (a) John Bardeen            (b) Walter Brattain
    (c) William Shockley        (d) all the above

18. Who, among the following list of Nobel Prize winners, got the award for Physics: Ernest Rutherford, Francis Aston, Walter Nernst, Peter Debye, Otto Hahn, Irving Langmuir, Glenn Seaborg, Frederick Soddy?
    (a) Rutherford, Aston and Otto Hahn
    (b) Nernst, Debye, Langmuir, Seaborg, Soddy
    (c) all the above
    (d) none of the above

19. Who among the following was awarded the Nobel Prize for Physics for his discoveries regarding the laws governing the radiation of heat?
    (a) Gustaf Kirchhoff          (b) Wilelm Wien
    (c) Ludwig Boltzmann       (d) Joseph Stefan

20. In 1933, the Nobel Prize for Physics was awarded to a German physicist for the creation of Quantum Mechanics. Who was he?
    (a) Werner Heisenberg      (b) Max Planck
    (c) Max Born                    (d) Erwin Schrödinger

# 21

# LITERATURE OF PHYSICS

It takes a great deal of history to produce a little literature.
— Henry James

1. *On the Revolution of the Celestial Orbs*, one of the earliest treatises on modern astronomy, describes a novel theory of the planetary system. Who was the author of this book, published posthumously?
   - (a) Plato
   - (b) Tycho Brahe
   - (c) Copernicus
   - (d) Kepler

2. *Micrographia* was the first book dealing with observations through a microscope. Who wrote it in 1665?
   - (a) Antono van Leeuwenhoek
   - (b) Robert Hooke
   - (c) Christiaan Huygens
   - (d) Leonardo da Vinci

3. Which of the following treatises first gave the description of the famous Bernoulli's theorem?
   - (a) *On Hydrostatics*
   - (b) *Treatise on Dynamics*
   - (c) *On the Equilibrium of Liquids*
   - (d) *Hydrodynamica*

4. *Perspectiva Communis,* a standard textbook for three centuries, was written by English scientist John Pecham around the year 1277. This book dealt with:
   (a) optics            (b) mechanics
   (c) magnetism      (d) astronomy

5. Who was the author of *De Stella Nova* (The New Star)?
   (a) Tycho Brahe
   (b) Blaise Pascal
   (c) Galileo Galili
   (d) D. Bernoulli

6. *Optica Promota* written by James Gregory in 1663 gave the first description of a:
   (a) reflecting telescope
   (b) refracting telescope
   (c) simple microscope
   (d) compound microscope

7. *Traité de L'Equilibré Des Liqueurs* (On the Equilibrium of Liquids), published posthumously, was written by:
   (a) Jean le Rond d'Alembert
   (b) Blaise Pascal
   (c) Edmé Mariotte
   (d) Robert Boyle

8. One of the great classical books of all time, *Philosophiae Naturalis Principia Mathematica* (The Mathematical Principle of Natural Philosophy), is better known as *Principia*. Which great scientist authored and published the same in 1687?
   (a) Andrew Motte      (b) Madame du Châtelet
   (c) Edmund Halley      (d) Sir Isaac Newton

9. *Reflexions Sur la Puissance du Feu* (On the Motive Power of Fire) was written in 1824 by a famous physicist–engineer, in which he established that heat and work are reversible conditions. Who was its author?
   (a) Hermann Ludwig von Helmholtz
   (b) Lord Kelvin
   (c) Rudolf Clausius
   (d) Nicolas 'Sadi' Carnot

10. Who is the author of the classic book *From Quarks to the Cosmos?*
    (a) Jack Steinberger
    (b) Melvin Schwartz
    (c) Antony Hewish
    (d) Leon Lederman

11. Prof. Jayant Vishnu Narlikar is not only an outstanding astrophysicist, but a popular science writer as well. Which of the following books has he written?
    (a) *The Nature of the Universe*
    (b) *Survey of the Universe*
    (c) *The Structure of the Universe*
    (d) *The Individual and the Universe*

12. Among many things that are common between Fred Hoyle and Jayant Narlikar is one of the following books that is jointly written by them. Name the book.
    (a) *Cosmology*
    (b) *Astronomy*
    (c) *Action at a Distance in Physics and Cosmology*
    (d) *The Nature of the Universe*

13. Though Albert Einstein did not get the Nobel Prize for his work on relativity theories, but the word 'relativity' has become synonymous with Einstein. Which of the following books on relativity has Einstein written?
    I.   *The Theory of Relativity*
    II.  *The Principle of Relativity*
    III. *The Meaning of Relativity*
    IV.  *The Special Theory of Relativity*
    V.   *Relativity: Special and General Theory*

    The correct combination is:
    (a) III and IV              (b) III and V
    (c) I and IV                (d) II and V

14. The Dewey Decimal Classification divides human knowledge in ten classes. Sciences come under 500. To which sub-division does Physics belong?
    (a) 510                     (b) 530
    (c) 540                     (d) 570

15. The famous book, *The Feynman Lectures on Physics,* is jointly written by:
    (a) Feynman, Leighton, and Sands
    (b) Feynman, Sands, and Gamow
    (c) Sands, Gamow, and Leighton
    (d) Leighton, Chaisson, and Hawking

16. Who is the author of *The Tao of Physics,* a fascinating book that draws parallels between modern physics and the Eastern Mysticism?
    (a) D.T. Suzuki
    (b) Lobsang Rampa
    (c) Lama Anagarika Govinda
    (d) Fritjof Capra

17. Which of the following wonderful books is written by the famous scientist Stephen Hawking?
    (a) *Encyclopedic Dictionary of Physics*
    (b) *How to Find Out in Physics*
    (c) *A Brief History of Time*
    (d) *The Nature of Time*

18. Who is the author of *Expanding Universe*?
    (a) Leon Lederman        (b) William Fowler
    (c) Arthur Eddington     (d) Antony Hewish

19. *Indian Journal of Physics* was founded in 1926. Who was its founder–editor?
    (a) C.V. Raman           (b) S.N. Bose
    (c) S. Chandrasekhar     (d) J.C. Bose

20. Which famous cosmologist is the author of *Black Holes and Body Universe*?
    (a) S. Chandrasekhar     (b) Stephen Hawking
    (c) Edward Appleton      (d) Arno Penzias

## 22

## BREAKTHROUGH

When you are courting a nice girl an hour seems like a second.
When you sit on a red-hot cinder a second seems like an hour.
That's relativity.

– A<small>LBERT</small> E<small>INSTEIN</small>

1. Which discovery in the field of Physics on 8 November
   1895 created a revolution in medical sciences?
   (a) radioactivity
   (b) X-rays
   (c) radioactive isotopes
   (d) nuclear magnetic resonance

2. Who, in 1888, produced and detected radiowaves for
   the first time?
   (a) Jagadish Chandra Bose (b) Guglielmo Marconi
   (c) Heinrich Hertz       (d) Lee de Forest

3. Who among the following physicists was the first to
   produce the artificial transmutation of elements in 1919?
   (a) Marie Curie
   (b) Ernest Oerlando Lawrence
   (c) Irene Joliot-Curie and Frederick Joliot
   (d) Ernest Rutherford

4. Which was the first planet to be discovered with the help of a telescope on 13 March 1781?
   (a) Uranus
   (b) Neptune
   (c) Saturn
   (d) Jupiter

5. Which discovery on 23 December 1947 created a revolution in every aspect of technology?
   (a) superconductivity      (b) laser
   (c) transistor             (d) computer

6. Albert Einstein's second paper on the Special Theory of Relativity established the famous formula $E = mc^2$. This formula infers that:
   (a) energy would be infinite if the mass disappears.
   (b) mass can be generated out of energy.
   (c) energy is directly proportional to the square of the velocity of light.
   (d) mass and energy are inter-convertible.

7. Which of the communication satellites provided the first live television between the United States, Europe, South America and Japan on 10 July 1962?
   (a) Telstar                (b) Early Bird
   (c) Inteleset-I            (d) Molniya

8. Dennis Gabor made a breakthrough in the field of image technology and was awarded the Nobel Prize in 1971. What did he invent?
   (a) Colour television
   (b) Holographic method of 3-dimensional imagery
   (c) Computerised graphics
   (d) Instant photography

9. Who was the first to discover that the electrical resistance of a conductor vanishes even before the absolute zero is attained?
   (a) Heike Kamerlingh-Onnes
   (b) L.N. Cooper
   (c) John Bardeen
   (d) Alex Müller

10. Pierre and Marie Curie discovered radioactivity after observing that thorium gives off these rays. Under what name were radioactive rays known at that time?
    (a) Bequerel rays
    (b) Uranium rays
    (c) Thorium rays
    (d) Curie rays

11. Michael Faraday and Joseph Henry independently discovered the phenomenon of electromagnetic induction in 1831. A year earlier, which famous principle did Henry discover before Faraday, but failed to get it published?
    (a) self-induction
    (b) transformer
    (c) induction coil
    (d) dynamo

12. Who was the first to liquify hydrogen?
    (a) Zygmund von Wrorlewski
    (b) Ludwig Edward Boltzmann
    (c) James Prescott Joule
    (d) Julius Robert Mayer

13. Name the US project that made the first atomic bomb?
    (a) Project Ozma         (b) Manhattan Project
    (c) Project Spartan      (d) Syncom Project

14. When only twenty-five, Albert Einstein published his revolutionary ideas through three scientific papers in quick succession in 1905. These papers were:
    I.   'On the Electrodynamics of Moving Bodies'
    II.  'The Quantum Law of the Emission and Absorption of Light'
    III. 'Does the inertia of a body depend on its energy content?'

    What is the order of publication of these papers?
    (a) I, II and III          (b) II, I and III
    (c) I, III and II          (d) III, I and II

15. Who was the first to visualise the unification of light and electromagnetism?
    (a) Sir James Jeans        (b) Thomas Young
    (c) James Clerk Maxwell    (d) Heinrich Hertz

16. Eye surgery is one of the medical procedures in which laser technology has become an important tool. Who, among the following, was the first to produce laser in 1960?
    (a) Theodore Maiman        (b) Charles Towns
    (c) Nikolai Basov          (d) Aleksandr Prochorov

17. He published a paper titled 'A Method of Reaching Altitudes', and shortly afterwards launched the first liquid-propellant rocket. Who was he?
    (a) Werner von Braun       (b) Robert Goddard
    (c) Charles Lindbergh      (d) Konstantin Tsiolkovsky

18. Which of the following phenomena was established by the discovery of photoelectric emission?
    (a) The quantum nature of light
    (b) The dual nature of matter
    (c) The corpuscular nature of light
    (d) The wave nature of light

19. Who was the director of the Manhattan Project for developing the first atomic bomb?
    (a) Enricc Fermi  (b) Albert Einstein
    (c) Robert Oppenheimer  (d) Arthur Crompton

20. A team of US physicists created the first controlled chain reaction in a pile of uranium and graphite at the University of Chicago on 2 December 1942. Who headed this team?
    (a) Robert Oppenheimer  (b) Otto Hahn
    (c) E.O. Lawrence  (d) Enrico Fermi

## 23

# END OF THE BEGINNING

> There was young lady named Bright,
> Whose speed was faster than light;
> She set out one day
> In a relative way,
> And returned home the previous night.
> — Arthur Buller

1.  The photograph shows a device orbiting the earth, which is able to 'see' farther than any telescope on earth. What is it called?

   (a) ROSAT, an X-ray satellite
   (b) The Gamma Ray Observatory
   (c) Hubble Space Telescope
   (d) The Cosmic Background Explorer

2. The Kamioka mine in Japan and the Homestake gold mine in South Dakota are famous for detecting:
   (a) heavy magnetic monopoles
   (b) neutrinos from stars and supernova
   (c) cosmic background radiations
   (d) gravitational waves

3. The world's largest and most powerful laser-fusion project is:
   (a) NOVA           (b) SHIVA
   (c) TOKAMAK        (d) ANTARES

4. Name the phenomenon predicted by Albert Einstein that is yet to be verified experimentally, and is caused by the rotation of the earth:
   (a) electrogravitation     (b) gravitoelectricity
   (c) magnetogravitation     (d) gravitomagnetism

5. What was Einstein's last 'dream'?
   (a) Verifying the existence of the gravitational waves.
   (b) Synthesising electromagnetism and nuclear forces.
   (c) Combining gravitational and nuclear forces.
   (d) Formulating a single unified field theory.

6. Out of the four fundamental forces, which one is not a 'part' of Grand Unification Theories (GUT)?
   (a) gravitational force
   (b) electromagnetic force
   (c) weak nuclear interaction
   (d) strong nuclear force

7. According to the General Theory of Relativity, which among the following waves propagate outward from their source and stretch and shrink space and matter?
   (a) gravitational waves     (b) electromagnetic waves
   (c) cosmic rays             (d) acoustic waves

8. According to the General Theory of Relativity:
   I. gravity is a force.
   II. gravity is the curvature of space–time.
   III. the planets follow the shortest path in the curved space–time about the sun.
   IV. in weak gravitational fields, Einstein's formulas yield the same answers as Newton's.

   Which combination is correct?
   (a) II and III only          (b) II and IV only
   (c) II, III and IV only       (d) I, II, III and IV

9. It is not a star but it emits tremendous amount of radiation of all wavelengths, and is the most energetic of all the heavenly bodies in the universe. What is it?
   (a) quasar                   (b) pulsar
   (c) supernova                (d) neutron star

10. Ephraim Fishbach discovered the hypercharge in 1986. What is this?
    (a) The fifth quark, Top or Truth.
    (b) The sixth quark, Bottom or Beauty.
    (c) The fifth fundamental force that acts counter to gravity.
    (d) The heaviest fundamental particle with spin 2.

11. Name the multi-billion dollar project, consisting of about 1500 radiotelescopes that may help detect extraterrestrial intelligent signal.
    (a) Project Cyclops          (b) Project Ozma
    (c) Project Manhattan        (d) Project ET

12. Based on advanced physics and medicine, the following are the three most powerful tools to scan the body:
   I.   CAT scanning
   II.  PET scanning
   III. MNR scanning

   Which combination makes use of X-rays?
   (a) I and III only          (b) I only
   (c) II and III only         (d) III only

13. Which of the following gives promise of producing a time measuring clock with an error of only one second in 33,000,000 years?
   (a) cesium atomic clock    (b) quartz crystal clock
   (c) helium laser            (d) hydrogen laser

14. The photograph shows the Great Nebula in Andromeda galaxy as seen through a powerful conventional telescope. On the right, an artist has drawn stars that might be seen with a 'special' telescope. What is this 'special' telescope?

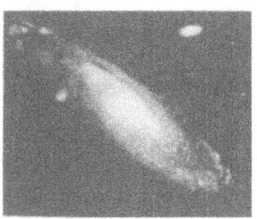

   (a) Hubble Space Telescope
   (b) Neutrino Telescope
   (c) Gamma Ray Telescope
   (d) Infra Ray Telescope

15. What is LIGO?
    (a) A project to detect the gravitational wave.
    (b) A project to gather signals from extra-terrestrial space.
    (c) The ultimate robot.
    (d) The ultimate superconductor.

16. P.A.M. Dirac hypothesised that the universal gravitation constant, G, was of a high magnitude at the beginning of the formation of the universe. Which of the following theories gives the variation of G with time, and thus threatening the General Theory of Relativity?
    (a) Hoyle–Narlikar theory
    (b) Brans–Dicke theory
    (c) Glashow–Salam theory
    (d) Chandrasekhar–Fowler theory

17. Name the thermal radiation having a temperature of about 3° K that is supposed to be uniformly distributed in the universe?
    (a) Cosmic microwave background radiation
    (b) Hawking radiation
    (c) Cosmic radiation
    (d) Microwave radiation

18. What is the name of the theory of electrically charged particles, like electrons and protons, and their interaction?
    (a) Quantum electronics
    (b) Quantum electrodynamics
    (c) Quantum electromagnetism
    (d) Relativistic quantum theory

19. A quantum field theory that combines the weak, strong, and electromagnetic interaction in a single theory with one symmetry group is called:
    (a) grand unified theory    (b) gauge theory
    (c) string theory            (d) super symmetry theory

20. What are the following:
    LEP I & II, HERA, SSC, TRISTAN I & II?
    (a) Futuristic models of spacecrafts
    (b) Chess computers
    (c) Latest set of particle accelerators in the form of colliders
    (d) Most distant quasars

# 24

# MISCELLANY

He doubted the existence of the Deity but accepted Carnot's cycle, and he had read Shakespeare and found him weak in chemistry.

– H.G. Wells

1. Among the following physicists, who excelled in writing poetry?
   I.   Alessandro Volta       II.  Lord Kelvin
   III. James Clerk Maxwell   IV. William Rankine

   Which combination is correct ?
   (a) I and II                (b) II and IV
   (c) all the above          (d) none of the above

2. In a state of depression, which of the following physicists committed suicide?
   (a) Ludwig Boltzmann       (b) Lev Landau
   (c) Henry Moseley          (d) Lise Meitner

3. Who among the following was the Physics adviser of Herr Hitler?
   (a) Johannes Stark         (b) Philipp Lenard
   (c) Wilhelm Wien           (d) Max von Laue

4. Once Albert Einstein described him as the artist in science. Who was he?
   (a) S.N. Bose          (b) Enrico Fermi
   (c) P.A.M. Dirac       (d) A.A. Michelson

5. What is common among the following physicists: Newton, Lord Kelvin, Herschel, Rutherford, J.J. Thomson?
   (a) All were buried in Westminster Abbey.
   (b) All were bachelors.
   (c) All were the first offspring of their parents.
   (d) All were born in England.

6. Read the following statements:
   I.   Astronomer Edwin Hubble studied law at Oxford University.
   II.  Physicist Victor de Broglie was a historian.
   III. Astronomer Nicolaus Copernicus took training in medicine.
   IV.  Physicist William Gilbert was a medical doctor.

   Which combination is correct?
   (a) I, II and III       (b) I, III and IV
   (c) none of the above   (d) all of the above

7. Masterminded by Dr Frank Drake in 1960, which was the first attempt to listen to broadcasts from extraterrestrial sources?
   (a) Project Cyclops     (b) Project Ozma
   (c) Project Manhattan   (d) Project Blue Book

8. Which famous poet wrote the following famous couplet in praise of Newton: 'Nature and Nature's laws lay hid in night:/God said "Let Newton be", and all was light'?
   (a) Alexander Pope      (b) William Wordsworth
   (c) Lord Byron          (d) Samuel Coleridge

9. A life-long friend of William Wordsworth, godfather of Michael Faraday, founder of philosophic alchemy, writer of non-science books like *Salmonia* and *Consolations in Travel,* and about whom once Samuel Coleridge said, 'The Man who born a Poet first converted poetry into Science'. Who was this famous scientist?
   (a) Joseph Henry
   (b) James Joule
   (c) Sir Humphry Davy
   (d) Thomas Young

10. Who among the following physicists was/were bachelor(s)?
   I.   Sir Isaac Newton
   II.  Robert Boyle
   III. Blaise Pascal

   Which combination is correct?
   (a) I and II
   (b) I and III
   (c) II and III
   (d) I, II and III

11. Which heavenly body among the following is worshipped as a powerful god: Inti by Peruvian Incas, Amen-ra by Egyptians, Phoebus-Apollo by Greeks, Surya Devata by Hindus?
   (a) Moon
   (b) Earth
   (c) Jupiter
   (d) Sun

12. Some scientists/astrologers link sun-spot cycles to political upheavals. Which of the following political revolution(s) occurred at times of maximum solar activity?
   I.   The American Revolution, 1776
   II.  The French Revolution, 1789
   III. The Russian Revolution, 1917

   Which is the correct combination?
   (a) I and II
   (b) II and III
   (c) I and III
   (d) I, II and III

13. Being citizens of the world, scientists are cosmopolitan in nature. Who, among the following, wrote in 1597, after being 'fired' to give up his rank as the leader of the Danish island of Hven, 'Everywhere the earth is below and the sky is above, and to the energetic man, every region is his fatherland.'?
    (a) Niccolo Tartaglia
    (b) Simon Stevinus
    (c) Tycho Brahe
    (d) Giovanni Battista Benedetti

14. If height of a man is 1 unit, the diameter of our galaxy is:
    (a) $10^{10}$              (b) $10^{20}$
    (c) $10^{30}$              (d) $10^{40}$

15. There are many incidents in the history of science relating to scientists being penalised and forced to give up publicly ideas conceived from logical thought or observations. Who among the following confessed: 'I abandon whatever in my book concerns the formation of earth and planets'?
    (a) Galileo Galilei
    (b) Georges-Louis Leclerc
    (c) Apollonius of Perga
    (d) Eratosthenes of Cyrene

16. Which famous artist among the following did experiments to study frictional force and gave empirical laws of static friction?
    (a) Paolo Uccello
    (b) Claude Lorrain
    (c) Leonardo da Vinci
    (d) Van Dyck

17. The two-way radio communications by private individuals as a leisure-time activity is called:
    (a) radio relay
    (b) Morse radio
    (c) ham radio
    (d) amateur communication

18. The type of vision for seeing with a minimum of light, as for owls and cats, is termed as:
    (a) photopic vision      (b) scotopic vision
    (c) foveal vision        (d) peripheral vision

19. What is 'coma'?
    (a) The visible head of a comet.
    (b) A plumblike distortion of spot of cathode ray tube
    (c) An aberration of a lens.
    (d) All mentioned in a, b, and c.

20. 'MORTALS, CONGRATULATE YOURSELVES THAT SO GREAT A MAN HAS LIVED FOR THE HONOUR OF THE HUMAN RACE'
    This inscription, translated from Latin, is written on the tombstone of which great physicist?
    (a) Michael Faraday       (b) Isaac Newton
    (c) Galileo Galilei       (d) Robert Boyle

## 25

# NEW PHYSICS

God does not play dice.

– ALBERT EINSTEIN

1.  The discovery of J/$\psi$ meson of mass 3097 MeV by Ting and Richter in 1974 gave the first indication of the existence of new quarks. Its studies have often been termed as:
    (a) New Philosophy      (b) New Science
    (c) End of Physics      (d) New Physics

2.  The gravitational forces inside a black hole pull matter towards it, thereby creating a domain where the existing laws of Physics break down. This domain is termed as:
    (a) spontaneous compactification
    (b) singularity
    (c) renormalisation
    (d) unitary symmetry

3.  What is the name of the massive particle, discovered in 1977, which is made from a bottom quark and bottom antiquark?
    (a) Upsilon      (b) Tao
    (c) Sigma      (d) Omega

4. The charge on a proton is +1, which in terms of the flavours of quarks is +2/3 + 2/3 − 1/3 (=1). Its quark composition is designated as:
   (a) ddu                    (b) uud
   (c) ssc                    (d) ccs

5. Name the particle whose quark composition is 'udd':
   (a) Omega minus            (b) pion
   (c) neutrino               (d) neutron

6. What is the study of the modern theory of the strong forces between quarks?
   (a) Quantum electrodynamics
   (b) Quantum electromagnetism
   (c) Quantum chromodynamics
   (d) Quantum hadronics

7. The boundary or surface surrounding a black hole having a property to trap the light rays is called:
   (a) Schwarzschild radius   (b) Chandrasekhar limit
   (c) world line             (d) event horizon

8. What do two quarks and two leptons form?
   (a) flavour                (b) colour
   (c) generation             (d) chaos

9. What name is given to the type of astronomy having the following characteristics:
   I.   It is carried out in the waveband 300nm to 10nm.
   II.  The atmosphere is opaque to the incoming radiation from space.
   III. Observations are to be carried out from above the earth's atmosphere.

   (a) Infra-red astronomy    (b) Ultra-violet astronomy
   (c) X-ray astronomy        (d) Gamma ray astronomy

10. The effective radius of a spherically symmetrical black hole is known as:
    (a) Schwarzschild radius
    (b) Kerr radius
    (c) Chandrasekhar radius
    (d) Rydberg radius

11. Name the philosophy according to which all events are completely determined by prior events?
    (a) astrology          (b) singularity
    (c) determinism        (d) chaos

12. The history of a particle in space–time is represented by:
    (a) world holes        (b) world line
    (c) alternative worlds (d) multiple worlds

13. Which of the following is the foremost place for the conduction of experiments on proton decay?
    (a) I.M.B. detector near Cleveland, Ohio
    (b) Kamioka Zinc Mine in Japan
    (c) Homestake Goldmine in South Dakota
    (d) Kolar Goldmine in Mysore, India

14. Taking quantum effects into consideration, the emission of particles produced by black hole which can be viewed as a kind of a pair of 'virtual' particles is known as:
    (a) cosmic radiation        (b) gravitational radiation
    (c) false radiation         (d) Hawking radiation

15. The maximum distance that a light signal could have travelled since the birth of the universe is called:
    (a) world line          (b) linear distance
    (c) horizon distance    (d) Hawking distance

16. The quantum particle that is resulted for a very short duration by the conversion of energy into mass according to the relation $E=mc^2$ is called:
    (a) virtual particle        (b) Higgs particle
    (c) W-particle             (d) Z-particle

17. The property of quarks that is like electronic charge but involves the strong force is called:
    (a) hadronic charge     (b) leptonic charge
    (c) virtual charge       (d) colour charge

18. Name the hypothetical particle, analogous to electric particles electron and proton, that carries an isolated north or south magnetic pole:
    (a) magnetic monopole  (b) magneton
    (c) magnetic dipole     (d) magnetic quantum

19. Name the radiation having a temperature of 3° k that is, supposed to be uniformly distributed in the universe:
    (a) Hawking radiation
    (b) Microwave background radiation
    (c) Cosmic radiation
    (d) Gravitational radiation

20. Who among the following Nobel Laureates is not associated with the theory of the unified weak and electromagnetic interaction between elementary particles?
    (a) Abdus Salam     (b) John Bardeen
    (c) Shelden Glashow  (d) Steven Weinberg

# ANSWERS

## 1. HISTORY OF PHYSICS

| | | | | |
|---|---|---|---|---|
| 1(b) | 2(a) | 3(d) | 4(c) | 5(a) |
| 6(d) | 7(d) | 8(c) | 9(a) | 10(d) |
| 11(a) | 12(c) | 13(c) | 14(b) | 15(a) |
| 16(d) | 17(a) | 18(c) | 19(b) | 20(a) |

## 2. FANTASIES OF THE MIND

| | | | | |
|---|---|---|---|---|
| 1(c) | 2(b) | 3(a) | 4(d) | 5(c) |
| 6(b) | 7(a) | 8(c) | 9(d) | 10(c) |
| 11(b) | 12(a) | 13(b) | 14(a) | 15(d) |
| 16(d) | 17(c) | 18(b) | 19(d) | 20(c) |

## 3. IDEAS IN ACTION

| | | | | |
|---|---|---|---|---|
| 1(d) | 2(c) | 3(b) | 4(a) | 5(b) |
| 6(c) | 7(a) | 8(d) | 9(c) | 10(b) |
| 11(d) | 12(b) | 13(a) | 14(d) | 15(c) |
| 16(d) | 17(b) | 18(c) | 19(c) | 20(d) |

## 4. MEASUREMENT AND UNITS

| | | | | |
|---|---|---|---|---|
| 1(d) | 2(a) | 3(a) | 4(c) | 5(b) |
| 6(c) | 7(b) | 8(d) | 9(d) | 10(c) |
| 11(a) | 12(a) | 13(b) | 14(b) | 15(a) |
| 16(d) | 17(a) | 18(d) | 19(c) | 20(d) |

## 5. SYMBOLIC PHYSICS: A TO Z

| | | | | |
|---|---|---|---|---|
| 1(a) | 2(b) | 3(a) | 4(c) | 5(b) |
| 6(c) | 7(d) | 8(d) | 9(b) | 10(a) |
| 11(d) | 12(c) | 13(d) | 14(c) | 15(c) |
| 16(d) | 17(b) | 18(c) | 19(a) | 20(a) |
| 16(c) | 17(c) | 18(d) | 19(b) | 20(c) |

## 6. CLASSICAL MECHANICS

| | | | | |
|---|---|---|---|---|
| 1(b) | 2(d) | 3(a) | 4(a) | 5(c) |
| 6(d) | 7(d) | 8(c) | 9(b) | 10(d) |
| 11(b) | 12(d) | 13(b) | 14(c) | 15(d) |
| 16(a) | 17(a) | 18(c) | 19(c) | 20(d) |

## 7. FIELDS AND FORCES

| | | | | |
|---|---|---|---|---|
| 1(c) | 2(a) | 3(a) | 4(c) | 5(b) |
| 6(d) | 7(a) | 8(c) | 9(b) | 10(a) |
| 11(b) | 12(d) | 13(c) | 14(a) | 15(c) |
| 16(a) | 17(d) | 18(c) | 19(d) | 20(a) |

## 8. ENERGY

| | | | | |
|---|---|---|---|---|
| 1(a) | 2(b) | 3(c) | 4(b) | 5(d) |
| 6(b) | 7(a) | 8(c) | 9(d) | 10(b) |
| 11(a) | 12(c) | 13(c) | 14(a) | 15(d) |
| 16(b) | 17(b) | 18(a) | 19(c) | 20(b) |

## 9. CAUSE AND EFFECT

| | | | | |
|---|---|---|---|---|
| 1(c) | 2(a) | 3(b) | 4(d) | 5(c) |
| 6(b) | 7(a) | 8(b) | 9(d) | 10(b) |
| 11(c) | 12(d) | 13(b) | 14(c) | 15(b) |
| 16(d) | 17(c) | 18(c) | 19(b) | 20(c) |

## 10. PHYSICAL PHENOMENA

| | | | | |
|---|---|---|---|---|
| 1(c) | 2(d) | 3(c) | 4(b) | 5(c) |
| 6(a) | 7(b) | 8(a) | 9(d) | 10(a) |
| 11(b) | 12(a) | 13(c) | 14(a) | 15(d) |
| 16(c) | 17(c) | 18(a) | 19(b) | 20(d) |

## 11. KITH AND KIN OF PHYSICS

| | | | | |
|---|---|---|---|---|
| 1(c) | 2(b) | 3(d) | 4(a) | 5(c) |
| 6(d) | 7(b) | 8(c) | 9(a) | 10(b) |
| 11(c) | 12(a) | 13(c) | 14(b) | 15(c) |
| 16(d) | 17(b) | 18(c) | 19(a) | 20(b) |

## 12. VIBRANT PHYSICS

| | | | | |
|---|---|---|---|---|
| 1(b) | 2(c) | 3(a) | 4(d) | 5(c) |
| 6(b) | 7(c) | 8(a) | 9(b) | 10(c) |
| 11(a) | 12(b) | 13(c) | 14(d) | 15(a) |
| 16(b) | 17(a) | 18(a) | 19(d) | 20(a) |

## 13. PROPERTIES OF MATERIALS

| | | | | |
|---|---|---|---|---|
| 1(b) | 2(c) | 3(a) | 4(b) | 5(d) |
| 6(c) | 7(d) | 8(b) | 9(a) | 10(b) |
| 11(d) | 12(a) | 13(b) | 14(d) | 15(b) |
| 16(a) | 17(b) | 18(a) | 19(d) | 20(d) |

## 14. MICROCOSMOS

| | | | | |
|---|---|---|---|---|
| 1(a) | 2(d) | 3(b) | 4(d) | 5(c) |
| 6(d) | 7(a) | 8(a) | 9(b) | 10(a) |
| 11(a) | 12(d) | 13(c) | 14(d) | 15(d) |
| 16(a) | 17(c) | 18(b) | 19(d) | 20(c) |

## 15. MACROCOSMOS

| | | | | |
|---|---|---|---|---|
| 1(c) | 2(b) | 3(a) | 4(d) | 5(a) |
| 6(c) | 7(b) | 8(c) | 9(a) | 10(d) |
| 11(c) | 12(b) | 13(c) | 14(a) | 15(b) |
| 16(c) | 17(d) | 18(b) | 19(a) | 20(c) |

## 16. LOGICAL PHYSICS

| | | | | |
|---|---|---|---|---|
| 1(d) | 2(b) | 3(d) | 4(b) | 5(c) |
| 6(a) | 7(d) | 8(d) | 9(b) | 10(c) |
| 11(d) | 12(a) | 13(c) | 14(c) | 15(a) |
| 16(b) | 17(b) | 18(c) | 19(a) | 20(c) |

## 17. CREATORS OF PHYSICS

| | | | | |
|---|---|---|---|---|
| 1(b) | 2(d) | 3(b) | 4(d) | 5(b) |
| 6(d) | 7(c) | 8(c) | 9(a) | 10(b) |
| 11(a) | 12(b) | 13(c) | 14(a) | 15(c) |
| 16(a) | 17(b) | 18(d) | 19(a) | 20(c) |

## 18. REASONING IN PHYSICS

| | | | | |
|---|---|---|---|---|
| 1(c) | 2(a) | 3(c) | 4(d) | 5(b) |
| 6(a) | 7(c) | 8(d) | 9(c) | 10(a) |
| 11(c) | 12(c) | 13(a) | 14(a) | 15(d) |
| 16(b) | 17(a) | 18(b) | 19(b) | 20(b) |

## 19. EXPERIMENTAL PHYSICS

| | | | | |
|---|---|---|---|---|
| 1(d) | 2(a) | 3(c) | 4(b) | 5(c) |
| 6(d) | 7(d) | 8(c) | 9(c) | 10(a) |
| 11(b) | 12(d) | 13(b) | 14(c) | 15(d) |
| 16(c) | 17(a) | 18(c) | 19(c) | 20(d) |

## 20. NOBEL PHYSICS

| | | | | |
|---|---|---|---|---|
| 1(c) | 2(b) | 3(a) | 4(b) | 5(d) |
| 6(a) | 7(c) | 8(b) | 9(d) | 10(d) |
| 11(a) | 12(c) | 13(d) | 14(a) | 15(d) |
| 16(b) | 17(d) | 18(d) | 19(b) | 20(a) |

## 21. LITERATURE OF PHYSICS

| | | | | |
|---|---|---|---|---|
| 1(c) | 2(b) | 3(d) | 4(a) | 5(c) |
| 6(a) | 7(b) | 8(d) | 9(d) | 10(d) |
| 11(c) | 12(c) | 13(b) | 14(b) | 15(a) |
| 16(d) | 17(c) | 18(c) | 19(a) | 20(b) |

## 22. BREAKTHROUGH

| | | | | |
|---|---|---|---|---|
| 1(b) | 2(c) | 3(d) | 4(a) | 5(c) |
| 6(d) | 7(a) | 8(b) | 9(a) | 10(b) |
| 11(d) | 12(a) | 13(b) | 14(b) | 15(c) |
| 16(a) | 17(b) | 18(a) | 19(c) | 20(d) |

## 23. END OF THE BEGINNING

| | | | | |
|---|---|---|---|---|
| 1(c) | 2(b) | 3(a) | 4(d) | 5(d) |
| 6(a) | 7(a) | 8(c) | 9(a) | 10(c) |
| 11(a) | 12(b) | 13(d) | 14(b) | 15(a) |
| 16(b) | 17(a) | 18(b) | 19(a) | 20(c) |

## 24. MISCELLANY

| | | | | |
|---|---|---|---|---|
| 1(c) | 2(a) | 3(a) | 4(d) | 5(a) |
| 6(d) | 7(b) | 8(a) | 9(c) | 10(d) |
| 11(d) | 12(b) | 13(c) | 14(b) | 15(a) |
| 16(c) | 17(c) | 18(b) | 19(d) | 20(b) |

## 25. NEW PHYSICS

| | | | | |
|---|---|---|---|---|
| 1(d) | 2(b) | 3(a) | 4(b) | 5(d) |
| 6(c ) | 7(d) | 8(c) | 9(b) | 10(a) |
| 11(c) | 12(b) | 13(a) | 14(d) | 15(c) |
| 16(a) | 17(d) | 18(a) | 19(b) | 20(b) |